THE
RECTORY UMBRELLA
AND
MISCHMASCH

by

LEWIS CARROLL

With a Foreword
by
FLORENCE MILNER
Harvard College Library

DOVER PUBLICATIONS, INC.
NEW YORK

This Dover edition, first published in 1971, is an unabridged and unaltered republication of the work originally published by Cassell & Company, Ltd., in 1932.

International Standard Book Number: 0-486-21345-5
Library of Congress Catalog Card Number: 70-166429

Manufactured in the United States of America
Dover Publications, Inc.
180 Varick Street
New York, N.Y. 10014

FOREWORD

"THE RECTORY UMBRELLA" and "Mischmasch," now, for the first time, published in full, are the last two of the eight manuscript magazines for which Charles Lutwidge Dodgson, as child and youth, was responsible. A footnote to the Preface in "The Rectory Umbrella" mentions only three earlier magazines, "Useful and Instructive Poetry," "The Rectory Magazine," and "The Comet." In the Preface to "Mischmasch" there is a detailed account of seven preceding ventures: "Useful and Instructive Poetry," "The Rectory Magazine," "The Comet," "The Rosebud," "The Star," "The Will-o'-the-Wisp," and "The Rectory Umbrella." "Mischmasch" brings the number up to eight. The first two are still in the possession of the family; the last two are in the Harcourt Amory Collection of Lewis Carroll in Harvard College Library, Cambridge, Massachusetts, U.S.A. So far as known, nothing of the intervening four has been preserved.

No one prophesied for the young editor any such wide popularity as he has attained, otherwise every scrap of this early work would have been carefully preserved. If anyone looked ahead, it was doubtless the father, who may have dreamed for this eldest son a brilliant career as a mathematician. But, as often happens, this son's claim to fame rests not upon any great achievement in his chosen work in mathematics, but upon the books he wrote merely for the pleasure of it—not upon his vocation but upon his avocation.

It was through editing these little magazines and doing most of the work upon them himself that he made his first semi-formal approach to literature and art. For the early magazines, it was the plan that all members of the family should contribute, but it was not long before the first enthusiasm wore off and Charles was left to carry on unaided. For "The Rectory Umbrella" he furnished all the material; for "Mischmasch" all except two poems.

In the Preface to "Mischmasch" is the statement, "'The Rectory Umbrella' was started, we believe, in 1849 or 1850, in a ready-bound square volume." This describes the ordinary exercise books used for the last two manuscripts. The preceding magazines evidently were issued in separate numbers and afterwards fastened together or crudely bound. He adds, "It was admired at the time but wholly unsupported and it took a year or more to fill the volume."

There are no dates to any of the articles in the book, but 1849 or 1850 places it probably in his last long vacation from Rugby, as, according to his diary, he left school on December 13, 1849. While no others of the family are represented, it still held their interest. That

vi

he began in a bound volume instead of on loose sheets as in the earlier ventures, indicates the increasingly personal attitude, although in content it followed, although more ambitiously, the idea of its predecessors.

Here are revealed many characteristics which became marked in the mature man. The extreme painstaking care which, in later life, he bestowed upon everything he did, is very evident. The originals are printed as carefully as the now famous " Alice's Adventures Underground," although in a slightly bolder hand, and the punctuation is meticulous. The scholarly atmosphere in which he lived is reflected in the many footnotes in " The Rectory Umbrella " which explain the text as minutely as though the document were a dissertation for the degree of Doctor of Philosophy. There are from one to a dozen on each page which, with humour or mock seriousness, explain the subject matter. Only a young person interested in mathematics would have thought of the footnotes on pages 9 and 14, although Charles did make a mistake in counting the ciphers for a nonillionth.

The amusing perversion of meaning in the titles of pretended engravings from pictures from the Vernon Gallery, and the illustrations of lines from famous poets, show the same type of humour that made the " Alice " books famous. The Vernon Gallery, in which he evidently was interested, was a collection of English paintings founded by a certain Robert Vernon at South Kensington. The collection was given to the National Gallery in 1847.

That Charles Dodgson had read widely both in lighter vein and in serious lines and that he was especially interested in poetry, is shown by familiar references to various authors—Milton, Gray, Shakespeare, Macaulay, Coleridge, Tennyson, Scott, Keats, Emerson, and others. By the same token may be traced his familiarity with *Punch* and *The Times*. History, music, politics, and science are also in evidence. Here he played the same sort of tricks upon words that later became a marked phase of his humour. In " Moans from the Miserable," the author probably made his first public appearance as a punster. His own enjoyment of the joke is shown in the footnote " readers ! observe the pun." In the second pun (page 18) he shows greater confidence in the reader, although he doubts the ability of the footman to see the joke. Here, too, is revealed his tendency to parodies which played such an important part in his published books. The best example is the really good parody on Horatius at the Bridge.

Here, too, appears his love for drawing which persisted through life. There is scarcely a page that has not one or more illustrations. Although Ruskin, in later years, discouraged Mr. Dodgson from devoting any time seriously to the idea of becoming an artist, these youthful illustrations, no matter how badly out of drawing, have action and do illustrate the text. This interest never entirely disappeared. He always kept close to his illustrators and his criticisms of the work of such artists as Tenniel, Furniss, Frost, and Holiday were frequent and insistent when they were illustrating his books. He usually succeeded in making them go his way.

"Mischmasch" belongs to his Oxford days, and reveals another stage of development. As dates for the various entries run from 1855 to 1862, the book must have been entirely written previous to his removal to Tom Quad, as he did not take possession of the suite there which he occupied until the end of his life, until 1868. He still harked back to the family magazines and, when he opened the new exercise book, had perhaps some idea of modelling it upon " The Rectory Umbrella." There is a decided resemblance in format although several points of departure in content. What it became eventually was a depository for such productions of his own and of other members of the family as he deemed worthy of preservation. The closest resemblance to its predecessor is in the drawings humorously illustrating quotations from the poets. It is noticeable, however, that the drawings are less abundant. Several pages are blank on which he had planned to put illustrations which were never added. The emphasis of the book is upon writing. With the exception of " The Mermaids," written by his sister Louisa, and " Blood," by his brother Wilfred, the literary efforts are limited to his own work. We find it, then, a combination scrap-book and common-place book.

The Preface, dated Croft, 1855, indicates its beginning during vacation. " The Two Brothers " (1853) and " The Mermaids " (1854) are salvage from an earlier time. Through page 35 all dates are either 1854 or 1855. After this nothing is dated until " Faces in the Fire " (1860). The last entry, " Bloggs' Woe," is of November, 1862. An increasing interest in poetry is manifest. " The Rectory Umbrella " contains but four poems : " Mischmasch," seventeen.

Mr. Collingwood, in " The Life and Letters of Lewis Carroll " and in " The Lewis Carroll Picture Book," has printed and reproduced several items from each of the two books, taking the greater number from " Misch-masch." Nothing in " The Rectory Umbrella " was considered by the author as worthy to be included in any of his later works, or for publication in any form. This is not true of " Mischmasch," for much of the material was used either before or after its appearance in the exercise book.

The most important entry in the book is " Stanza from Anglo-Saxon Poetry," which appeared nearly fifteen years later in " Through the Looking-Glass " as the first stanza of " Jabberwocky," exactly as it stands here. The explanation of the meanings of the strange words also parallels that given by Humpty Dumpty. " She's all my fancy painted him " was rewritten and admitted in evidence at the trial of the Knave of Hearts in " Alice in Wonderland." " The Three Voices " appeared in " The Train," a magazine to which Lewis Carroll contributed during its brief existence, in the issue of November, 1856, and in the first edition of " Phantasmagoria " (1883). The original in " Misch-masch " had twenty-eight stanzas in each of the three parts. When published, the number was increased and several verbal changes made. " Melancholetta," " Ode to Damon," " Lines," and " Bloggs' Woe " all appeared in " College Rhymes," of which Lewis Carroll was for a time editor. All but " Ode to Damon " were included in " Phantasmagoria " with some changes. " Bloggs' Woe " was changed to " Size and Tears," and the name Bloggs to Brown. " Lines " was re-named " A Valentine."

The scrap-book idea is carried out through the insertion of several newspaper clippings pasted in. Not all of them are credited to the publication in which they were printed. Chapter III of " Wilhelm von Schmitz " is a newspaper clipping from the *Whitby Gazette*. Chapter IV is in the author's characteristic printing hand. The first two chapters are missing here, but Mr. Langford Reed, in " Further Nonsense," has printed the story in full as it appeared in the *Whitby Gazette*.

In the review, " Photographic Exhibition," a clipping from the *Illustrated News* of January 28, 1860, is the suggestion that Mr. Dodgson was already deep in photography, which later became an absorbing pastime.

To sum up, we find in these two early manuscript books many interests that matured and were emphasized in later years : writing, a keen sense of humour shown through his skill in playing with words, drawing, music, photography, mathematics, and even science. In all these the future Lewis Carroll is foreshadowed.

FLORENCE MILNER.

HARVARD COLLEGE LIBRARY,
    CAMBRIDGE, MASSACHUSETTS,
        U.S.A.

CONTENTS

THE RECTORY UMBRELLA

PREFACE

WE venture once more before the Public, hoping to receive the same indulgence and support which has been hitherto bestowed on our Editorial efforts. Our success in former Magazines [1] has been decided : each has been more admired than its predecessor, and the last, the Comet, has been so universally believed to be the *ne plus ultra* of magazines, that we believe the only thing which can put an end to the delusion will be the issue of the Umbrella. We now in full confidence enter on our present duties.—EDITOR.

THE WALKING-STICK OF DESTINY

Ch. 1.

THE Baron was pacing his tapestried chamber two mortal hours ere sunrise.[2] Ever and anon he would pause at the open casement, and gaze from its giddy height [3] on the ground beneath. Then a stern smile [4] would light up his gloomy brow, and muttering to himself in smothered accents, " 'twill do " he would again resume his lonely march.

Uprose the glorious sun, and illumined [5] the dark-

---

[1] Viz: the Rectory Magazine and the Rectory Comet. The " R.M." succeeded " Useful and instructive Poetry."

[2] i.e., probably at about 3 o'clock in the morning.

[3] 10 feet, vide page 28.   [4] Vide page 4.   [5] Illuminated.

ened world with the light of day : still was the haughty Baron pacing his chamber, albeit his step was hastier and more impatient than before, and more than once he

stood motionless, listening anxiously and eagerly, then turned with a disappointed air upon his heel, while a darker shade passed over his brow. Suddenly the trumpet [1] which hung at the castle gate gave forth a shrill [2] blast : the Baron heard it, and savagely beating his breast with both his clenched fists, he murmured in bitter tone " the time draws nigh, I must nerve myself for action." Then, throwing himself into an easy chair, he hastily drank [3] off the contents of a large goblet of wine which stood on the table, and in vain attempted to assume an air of indifference. The door was suddenly thrown open and in a loud voice an attendant announced " Signor Blowski ! "

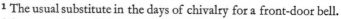

[1] The usual substitute in the days of chivalry for a front-door bell.
[2] So as to be audible at a greater distance.
[3] Drinking wine was his constant occupation.

"Be seated! Signor! you are early this morn, and Alonzo! ho! fetch a cup of wine for the Signor! spice [1] it well, boy! ha! ha! ha!" and the Baron laughed loud and boisterously, but the laugh was forced and hollow,[2] and died quickly away. Meanwhile the stranger, who had not uttered a syllable, carefully divested himself of his hat and gloves,[3] and seated himself opposite to the Baron, then having quietly waited till the Baron's laughter had subsided, he commenced in a harsh grating tone, "The Baron Muggzwig greets you, and sends you this"; why did a sudden paleness overspread the Baron Slogdod's features? why did his fingers tremble, so that he could scarcely open the letter? for one moment he glanced at it, and then raising his head, "Taste the wine, Signor," he said in strangely altered tone, "regale yourself, I pray," handing him one of the goblets which had just been brought in.

The Signor received it with a smile, put his lips to it, and then quietly changing goblets with the Baron without his perceiving it, swallowed half the contents at a draught. At that moment Baron Slogdod looked up, watched him for a moment as he drank, and smiled the smile of a wolf.[4]

[1] Hot spiced wine was much drunk in those days, vide page 17.
[2] The voice was sometimes hollow as well as the laugh, vide page 41.
[3] Vide his exit without either, next page.
[4] With most probably an hyena's laugh.

3

For full ten minutes there was a dead silence through the apartment, and then the Baron closed the letter, and raised his face : their eyes met : the Signor had many a time faced a savage tiger at bay without flinching, but now he involuntarily turned away his eyes. Then did the Baron speak in calm and measured tone: " You know, I presume, the contents of this letter ? " the Signor bowed, " and you await an answer ? " " I do." " *This*, then, is my answer," shouted the Baron, rushing upon him, and in another moment he had precipitated him from the open window. He gazed after him for a few seconds as he fell, and then tearing up the letter which lay on the table into innumerable pieces, he scattered them to the wind.

(*Continued at* page 8.)

4

Yᴇ FATALLE CHEYSE

I

Yᴛᴛᴇ wes a mirke an dreiry cave,
  Weet scroggis [1] owr ytte creepe,
Gurgles withyn yᵉ flowan wave
  Throw channel braid an deip.

2

Never withyn that dreir recesse
  Wes sene yᵉ lyghte of daye,
Quhat bode azont [2] yt's mirkinesse [3]
  Nane kend an nane mote saye.

3

Yᵉ monarche rade owr brake an brae,
  An drave yᵉ yellynge packe,
Hiz meany [4] au', richte cadgily,[5]
  Are wendynge [6] yn hiz tracke.

4

Wi' eager iye, wi' yalpe an crye
  Yᵉ hondes yode [7] down yᵉ rocks :
Ahead of au' their companye
  Renneth yᵉ panky [8] foxe.

5

Yᵉ foxe hes soughte that cave of awe,
  Forewearied [9] wi' hiz rin,
Quha nou ys he sae bauld an braw [10]
  To dare to enter yn ?

6

Wi' eager bounde hes ilka honde
  Gane till that caverne dreir,
Fou [11] many a yowl [12] ys [13] hearde arounde,
  Fou [11] many a screech of feir.

---

[1] Bushes.   [2] Beyond.   [3] Darkness.
[4] Company.   [5] Merrily.
[6] Going, journeying.   [7] Went.
[8] Cunning.   [9] Much wearied.   [10] Brave.
[11] Full.   [12] Howl.   [13] Is.

7

Like ane wi' thirstie appetite
  Quha swalloweth orange pulp,
Wes hearde a huggle an a bite,
  A swallow an a gulp.

8

Ye kynge hes lap frae aff hiz steid,
  Outbrayde [1] hiz trenchant brande ;
" Quha on my packe of hondes doth feed,
  Maun deye benead thilke hande."

9

Sae sed, sae dune : ye stonderes [2] hearde
  Fou many a mickle [3] stroke,
Sowns [4] lyke ye flappynge of a birde,
  A struggle an a choke.

10

Owte of ye cave scarce fette [5] they ytte,
  Wi pow [6] an push an hau' [7]—
Whereof Y've drawne a littel bytte,
  Bot durst nat draw ytte au. [8]

---

[1] Drawn.   [2] Bystanders.   [3] Heavy.
[4] Sounds.   [5] Fetch.   [6] Pull.   [7] Haul.
[8] All.

SIR J. REYNOLDS. PAINTER.

F. JOUBERT. ENGRAVER.

THE AGE OF INNOCENCE.
from the picture in the Vernon Gallery.

THE VERNON GALLERY

As our readers will have seen by the preceding page, we have commenced engraving the above series of pictures. "The Age of Innocence," by Sir J. Reynolds, representing a young Hippopotamus seated under a shady tree, presents to the contemplative mind a charming union of youth and innocence.— EDITOR.

THE WALKING-STICK OF DESTINY
Ch. 2.

"ONE! two! three!" The magician set down the bottle, and sank exhausted into a seat: "Nine weary hours," he sighed, as he wiped his smoking brow, "nine weary hours have I been toiling, and only got to the eight-hundred and thirty-second ingredient! a-well! I verily believe Martin Wagner [1] hath ordered three drops of everything on the face of this earth in his prescription. [2]   However there are only

[1] This celebrated individual was born at Stockholm in 1548.
[2] Probably some magic charm.

a hundred and sixty-eight [1] ingredients more to put in
—'twill soon be done—then comes the seething [2]—
and then——" He was checked in his soliloquy by a
low timid rap outside: " 'Tis Blowski's knock," muttered the old man, as he slowly undid the bars and
fastenings of the door, " I marvel what brings *him* here
at this late hour. He is a bird [3] of evil omen: I do
mistrust his vulture face.[4]—Why! how now, Signor?"
he cried, starting back in surprise as his visitor entered,
" where got you that black eye? and verily your face
is bruised like any rainbow![5] who has insulted you? or
rather," he muttered in an undertone, " whom have you
been insulting, for that were the more likely of the two."

" Never mind my face, good father," hastily answered
Blowski, " I only tripped up, coming home last night
in the dark, that's all, I do assure you. But I am now
come on other business—I want advice—or rather I
should say I want your opinion—on a difficult question—suppose a man was to—suppose two men—suppose there were two men, A and B [6]——" " suppose!

[1]   From 1000 ingredients
         subtract 832
         ————
and there remain   168 more to put in.

[2] Boiling.   [3] We have a similar expression " a jail-bird."

[4] This the artist has not ventured to depict.

[5] Viz: violet, indigo, blue, green, yellow, orange, red.

[6] By this idea he clearly showed his great mathematical turn of
mind.

9

suppose ! " contemptuously muttered the magician, " and suppose these men, good father, that is A, was to bring B a letter, then we'll suppose A read the letter, that is B, and then B tried—I mean A tried—to poison B—I mean A [1]—and then suppose "—" My son," here interposed the old man, " is this a general case you are putting ? Methinks you state it in a marvellously confused manner." " *Of course* it's a general case," savagely answered Blowski, " and if you'd just listen instead of interrupting, methinks you'd understand it better ! " " Proceed, my son," mildly replied the other.

" And then suppose A—that is B—threw A out of the window—or rather," he added in conclusion, being himself by this time a little confused, " or rather I should have said the other way." The old man rubbed his beard,[2] and mused for some time: " Aye, aye," he said at length, " *I* see, A — B — so so[3]—B poisons

[1] His confusion was caused by the consciousness that he was telling falsehoods.

[2] An action symbolical of deep thought.

[3] Meaning, " yes, yes."

A—" "No! no!" cried the signor, "B *tries* to poison A, he didn't really do it, I changed the—I mean," he hastily added, turning crimson as he spoke, "you're to *suppose* that he doesn't really do it." "Aye!" continued the magician, "it's all clear *now*—B—A—to be sure—but what has all this to do with your cut[1] face?" he suddenly asked. "Nothing whatever," stammered Blowski, "I've told you once that I cut my face by a fall from my horse—" "Ah! well! let's see," repeated the other in a low voice, "tripped up in the dark—fell from his horse—hm! hm!—yes, my lad, *you're* in for it—I should say," he continued in a louder voice, "it were better—but troth I know not yet what the question is." "Why, what had B better do," said the signor. "But who is B?" inquired the magician, "standeth B for Blowski?" "No," was the reply, "I meant A." "Oh!" returned he, "*now* I perceive—but verily I must have time to consider it, so adieu, fair[2] sir," and, opening the door he abruptly showed his visitor out: "And now," said he to himself, "for the mixture—let me see—three drops of—yes, yes, my lad, *you're* in for it."[3]

(*Continued at page* 16.)

[1] And bruised, vide page 4.   [2] Spoken ironically.
[3] Vide page 41.

MOANS FROM THE MISERABLE,[1]
OR THE WRETCH'S WAIL

PITIFUL SIRS,

We, the undersigned victims of unfeeling, heartless barbarity, entreat you of your pitifulness to "lend an ear," as the poet saith : alack ! we would not have you give it, knowing the treatment our own are subject to. Our owners, or guardians, we know not which they be, declare that they love us, but ah ! it must be as Isaak Walton loved the frog, for the essence of their love is cruelty. In proof of this love they do daily bear us about by our ears, kind sirs ; mine tingle even to think of it, they do put us down, do catch us up again, do whirl us round, and do howl into our ears words of affection and endearment, the very recollection whereof maketh us to shudder :

> "Oh ye whose hearts have nerves,
> Oh ye whose eyes have tears,
> It is not your love you are wearing out,
> But living victim's ears ! "

So, an *ear*nest [2] Adieu,
> from your h*ear*t-wrung victims,
>> The Loved and Tortured.

[1] The real authors were the Rectory rabbits.
[2] Reader ! pray observe the pun.

12

J. F. HERRING PAINTER

E. KACNBA ENORAVER.

THE SCANTY MEAL.
from the picture in the Vernor Gallery.

THE VERNON GALLERY
"THE SCANTY MEAL"

WE have been unusually [1] successful in our second engraving from the Vernon Gallery. The picture is intended, as our readers will perceive, to illustrate the evils of homœopathy.[2] This idea is well carried out through the whole picture. The thin old lady at the head of the table is in the painter's best style : we almost fancy we can trace in the eye of the other lady a lurking suspicion that her glasses are not really in fault, and that the old gentleman has helped her to *nothing* instead of a nonillionth.[3] Her companion has evidently got an empty glass in his hand : the two children in front are admirably managed, and there is a sly smile on the footman's face, as if he thoroughly enjoyed either the bad news he is bringing, or the wrath of his mistress. The carpet is executed with that elaborate care for which Mr. Herring is so famed, and the picture on the whole is one of his best.

[1] Perhaps an incorrect expression, as it was only the second attempt.

[2] The science of taking medicine in infinitely small doses.

[3] $\dfrac{1}{1000000000000000000000000000000}$

ZOOLOGICAL PAPERS

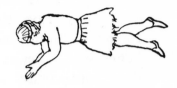

NO. I.
PIXIES

THE origin of this curious race of creatures is not at present known: the best description we can collect of them is this, that they are a species of fairies about two feet high,[1] of small and graceful figure; they are covered with a dark reddish sort of fur; the general expression of their faces is sweetness and good humour; the former quality is probably the reason why foxes are so fond of eating them. From Coleridge we learn the following additional facts; that they have "filmy pinions," something like dragon flies' wings, that they " sip the furze-flower's fragrant dew " (that, however, could only be for breakfast, as it would dry up before dinner time), and they are wont to " flash their faery feet in gamesome prank," or, in more common language, " to dance the polka [2] like winking."

From an old English legend [3] which, as it is familiar to most of our readers, we need not here repeat, we

---

[1] So they are described by the inhabitants of Devonshire, who occasionally see them.

[2] Or any other step.

[3] A tradition, introduced into notice by the Editor.

15

learn that they have a strong affection for raw turnips, decidedly a more vulgar sort of food than "fragrant dew"; and from their using churns and kettles we conjecture that they are not unacquainted with tea, milk, butter &cc. They are tolerably good architects, though their houses must unavoidably have something the appearance of large dog kennels, and they go to market occasionally, though from what source they get the money [1] for this purpose, has hitherto remained an unexplained mystery. This is all the information we have been able to collect on this interesting subject. In our next paper we propose to discuss the natural history of "the Lory." (*Continued at page* 23.)

THE WALKING-STICK OF DESTINY
Ch. 3.

IT had struck twelve o'clock two minutes and a quarter. The Baron's footman [2] hastily seized a large goblet,[3] and gasped with terror as he filled it with hot, spiced wine. " 'Tis past the hour, 'tis past," he groaned in anguish, " and surely I shall now get the red hot poker the Baron hath so often promised me, oh !

[1] Vide a similar difficulty, page 50.
[2] Or attendant, vide page 2.
[3] The Baron's meals seem to have consisted of nothing but hot, spiced wine. Hence his fiery temper.

woe is me! would that I had prepared the Baron's lunch [1] before!" and, without pausing a second he grasped in one hand the steaming goblet and flew along the lofty passages with the speed of a race horse. In less time than we take to relate it he reached the Baron's door, and— tiptoe, not  apartment, opened the remained standing on daring to move one way or the other, petrified with utter astonishment. "Now

---

[1] The very footman calls wine his "lunch." We *know* that he breakfasted on it, see page 2.

then! donkey!" roared the Baron, "why stand you there staring your eyes out like a great toad [1] in a fit of apoplexy?" (the Baron was remarkably choice in his similes:) "what's the matter with you? speak out! can't you?"

The unfortunate domestic made a desperate effort to speak, and managed at length to get out the words "Noble Sir!" "Very good! that's a very good beginning!" said the Baron in a rather pacified tone for he liked being called "noble," "go ahead! don't be all day about it!" "Noble Sir!" stammered the alarmed man, "where—where—ever—is—the stranger?" "*Gone!*" said the Baron sternly and emphatically, pointing unconsciously his thumb over his right shoulder, "gone! he had other visits to pay, so he *condescended* [2] to go and pay them—but where's my wine?" he abruptly asked, and his attendant was only too glad to place the goblet in his hands, and get out of the room.

The Baron drained the goblet at a draught,[3] and then walked to the window: his late victim was no longer to be seen, but the Baron, gazing on the spot where he had fallen muttered to himself with a

[1] It is doubtful whether the Baron thought him most like a donkey or a toad.

[2] A pun which the footman could not have understood.

[3] Vide page 2.

stern[1] smile, "Methinks I see a dint[2] in the ground." At that moment a mysterious looking figure[3] passed by, and the Baron, as he looked after him, could not help thinking "I wonder who that is!" long time he gazed after his retreating footsteps, and still the only thought which rose to his mind was "I do wonder who that is!"

(*Continued at page 25.*)

THE STORM

I

An old man sat anent a clough,[4]
  A grizzed[5] old man an' weird,[6]
Deep were the wrinks in his aged brow,
  An' hoar his snowy beard,
All tremmed[7] before his glance, I trow,[8]
  Sae savagely he leared.

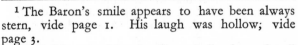

---

[1] The Baron's smile appears to have been always stern, vide page 1. His laugh was hollow; vide page 3.
[2] Probably caused by the Signor's "vulture face," vide page 9.
[3] Vide page 28.   [4] Probably a bank.   [5] Grizzled.
[6] Wizard-like.   [7] Trembled.
[8] = I wot, I ween, meaning nearly the same as "I know."

2

The rain cloud cam frae out the west,
   An' spread athwart [1] the sky,
The crow has cowered [2] in her nest,
   She kens the storm is nigh,
He folds his arms across his breast,
Thunder an' lightning do your best!
   "I will not flinch nor fly!"

3

Draggles [3] with wet the tall oak tree,
   Beneath the dashing rain,
The old man sat, an' gloomily
   He gazed athwart the plain,
Down on the wild and heaving sea,
Where heavily an' toilsomely
   Yon vessel ploughs the main.

4

Above the thunder cloud frowns black,
   The dark waves howl below,
Scarce can she hold along her track,
   Fast rocking to an' fro,
And oft the billow drives her back,
And oft her straining timbers crack,
   Yet onward she doth go.

5

The old man gazed without a wink,
   An' with a deadly [4] grin:
"I laid a wager she would sink,
   Strong hopes had I to win;
'Twas ten to one, but now I think,
   That Bob will sack the tin." [5]
Then from the precipice's brink
   He plunged headforemost in.[6]

---

[1] Across. [2] Crouched. [3] Hangs heavily.
[4] Or, murderous. [5] Pocket the money.
[6] Imitated from the conclusion of Gray's
"Bard," only finer.

W. COLLINS. PAINTER.

C. COUSEN. ENGRAVER.

THE WOODLAND GAIT.

From the picture in the Vernon Gallery.

THE VERNON GALLERY
"THE WOODLAND GAIT"

THIS charming picture represents a country dance : the intention of the painter is to pourtray rustic manners, untaught and unpolished ; in this aim he has succeeded admirably, for surely no one would suppose either of the couple in the foreground had ever figured at a London ball.

The little man, bounding up at least a foot from the ground, evidently prides himself a good deal on his agility, but his partner, if one may judge by the smirk on her face, considers her own style of dancing more elegant and graceful. There is an expression of energy in the fiddler's face as though he threw his whole life into the fiddle bow, and the languishing flute-player is evidently some would-be Mozart,[1] whom the bad taste and bad ear of his unmusical neighbours has hitherto prevented from rising into celebrity. The rustic gait of all the four figures is, in our opinion, admirably depicted.

[1] " Some mute inglorious Milton here may rest,
Some Cromwell, guiltless of his country's blood."
Gray's *Elegy*.

ZOOLOGICAL PAPERS

NO. 2:

THE LORY

THIS creature is, we believe, a species of parrot : Southey informs us that it is a " bird of gorgeous plumery," [1] and it is our private opinion that there never existed more than one, whose history as far as practicable we will now lay before our readers.

The time and place of the Lory's birth is uncertain : the egg from which it was hatched was most probably, to judge from the colour of the bird, one of those magnificent Easter eggs [2] which our readers have doubtless often seen ; the experiment of hatching an Easter egg is at any rate worth trying.

That it came into the possession of Cambeo, or Cupid, at a very early age, is evident from its extreme docility, as we find him using it, by all accounts without saddle or bridle,[3] for a kind of shooting pony in Southey's poem of " the Curse of Kehama." We need not relate its history therein contained, as our readers may see it themselves, so we proceed at once to the conclusion. When Kehama had done for the rest of the gods, and had been thereupon scorched by the combined influence

[1] Plumage, feathers.

[2] Of these a full description may be found in the sixth number of the " Comet."

[3] A bridle would be useless.

23

of Seeva's angry eye, and the Amreeta drink, which must have been something like fluid curry powder, it is more than probable that in the universal smash which then occurred, Cambeo's affairs among others were wound up. His goods and chattels were then most likely put up to auction, the Lory included, which we have reason to believe was knocked down to the Glendoveer,[1] in whose possession it remained for the rest of its life.

After its death we conjecture that the Glendoveer, unwilling to lose sight of its " plumery," had it stuffed, and some years afterwards, at the suggestion of Kailyal, presented it to the Museum at York, where it may now be seen, by the inquiring reader, admittance one shilling. Having thus stated all we know, and a good deal we don't know, on this interesting subject, we must conclude : our next subject will probably be " Fishs."

(*Continued at page* 33.)

[1] A happy spirit with large blue wings like an Aerial Machine.

THE WALKING-STICK OF DESTINY
Ch. 4.

DOWN went the western sun, and darkness was already stealing [1] over the earth when for the second [2] time that day the trumpet which hung at the Baron's gate was blown. Once more did the weary domestic ascend to his master's apartment, but this time it was a stranger whom he ushered in, "Mr. Milton Smith"! The Baron hastily rose from his seat at the unwonted [3] name, and advanced to meet his visitor.

"Greetings fair, noble sir," commenced the illustrious visitor, in a pompous tone and with a toss [4] of the head, "it betided me to hear of your name and abode, and I made high resolve to visit and behold you ere night!" "Well, fair sir, I hope you are satisfied with the sight," interrupted the Baron, wishing to cut short a conversation he neither understood nor liked. "It rejoiceth me," was the reply,

[1] Expressive of its slow and imperceptible advance.
[2] Vide page 2.
[3] And "unwanted" too, as we afterwards learn.
[4] Vide illustration.

"nay, so much so that I could wish to prolong the pleasure, for there is a Life and Truth [1] in those tones which recall to me scenes of earlier days—" "Does it indeed?" said the Baron, considerably puzzled. "Ay soothly," returned the other; "and now I bethink me," walking to the window, "it was the country likewise I did desire to look upon; 'tis fine, is't not?" "It's a very fine country," [2] replied the Baron, adding internally, "and I wish you were well out of it!"

The stranger stood some minutes gazing out of the window, and then said, suddenly turning to the Baron, "You must know, fair sir, that I am a poet!" "Really?" replied he, "and pray what's that?" Mr. Milton Smith made no reply, but continued his observations, "Perceive you, mine host, the enthusiastic [3] halo which encircles yon tranquil mead?" "The quickset hedge, you mean," remarked the Baron rather contemptuously, as he walked up to the window. "My mind," continued his guest, "feels alway a bounding —and a longing—for—what is True and Fair [4] in Nature, and—and—see you not the gorgeous rusticity —I mean sublimity, which is wafted over, and as it were intermingled with the verdure—that is, you know, the

[1] Dickens' style.
[2] i.e. by daylight, it was now growing dark.
[3] Reason sacrificed to poetry.
[4] Vide note (1), an imitation, but superior.

grass?" "Intermingled with the grass? oh! you mean the buttercups [1]?" said the other, "yes, they've a very pretty effect." "Pardon me," replied Mr. Milton Smith, "I meant not that, but—but I could almost poetise thereon!

> "Lovely meadow, thou whose fragrance
> Beams beneath the azure sky,

"Where repose the lowly—" "Vagrants," [2] suggested the Baron: "Vagrants!" repeated the poet, staring with astonishment, "Yes, vagrants, gipsies you know," coolly replied his host, "there are very often some sleeping down in the meadow." The inspired [3] one shrugged his shoulders, and went on

"Where repose the lowly violets," "Violets doesn't rhyme half as well as vagrants," argued the Baron. "Can't help that," was the reply:

"Murmuring gently"—"oh my eye!" [2] said the Baron, finishing the line for him, "so there's one stanza done, and now I must wish you good night; you're welcome to a bed, so, when you've done poetising, ring the bell, and the servant will show you where to sleep." "Thanks," replied the poet, as the Baron left the room.

[1] A sign of bad land, and as it was the Baron's estate, we may guess from this that he was not rich. A further proof of this may be found in page 58.

[2] The Baron had evidently a good ear for rhyme.

[3] Quasi-inspired.

"Murmuring gently with a sigh—Ah! *that's* all right," he continued when the door was shut, and leaning out of the window he gave a low whistle. The mysterious figure in a cloak immediately emerged[1] from the bushes, and said in a whisper, " All right ? " " *All right*," returned the poet, " I've sent the old covey[2] to sleep with some poetry, by the bye I nearly forgot that stanza you taught me, I got into *such* a fix ! However the coast is clear now, so look sharp." The figure then produced a rope ladder from under his cloak, which the poet proceeded to draw up.

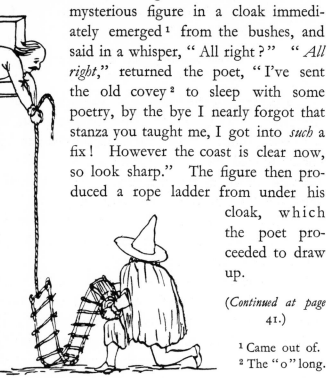

(*Continued at page* 41.)

[1] Came out of.
[2] The " o " long.

SIR. D. WILKIE. PAINTER.

W. GREATBACH. ENGRAVER.

THE FIRST EARRING.

From the picture in the Vernon Gallery

THE VERNON GALLERY
"THE FIRST EARRING"

THE scene from which this excellent picture is painted is taken from a passage in the autobiography [1] of the celebrated Sir William Smith [2] of his life when a schoolboy : we transcribe the passage : " One day Bill Tomkins [3] and I were left alone in the house, the old doctor being out : after playing a number of pranks Bill laid me a bet of sixpence that I wouldn't pour a bottle of ink over the Doctor's cat. *I did it*, but at that moment old Muggles came home, and caught me by the ear as I attempted to run away. My sensations at the moment I shall never forget ; *on that occasion I received my first earring.*[4] The only remark Bill made to me, as he paid me the money afterwards was, " I say, didn't you just howl jolly ! " The engraving is an excellent copy of the picture.

[1] A man's history of his own life.
[2] The author of " the Bandy-legged Butterfly."
[3] Afterwards President of the Society for the prevention of Cruelty to Animals.
[4] Or a pulling by the ear.

DIFFICULTIES

N O. I.

HALF of the world, or nearly so, is always in the light of the sun : as the world turns round, this hemisphere of light shifts round too, and passes over each part of it in succession.

Supposing on Tuesday it is morning at London ; in another hour it would be Tuesday morning at the west of England ; if the whole world were land we might go on tracing [1] Tuesday Morning, Tuesday Morning all the way round, till in 24 hours we get to London again. But we *know* that at London 24 hours after Tuesday morning it is Wednesday morning. Where then, in its passage round the earth, does the day change its name ? where does it lose its identity ?

Practically there is no difficulty in it, because a great part of its journey is over water, and what it does out at sea no one can tell : and besides there are so many different languages that it would be hopeless to attempt to trace the name of any one day all round. But is the case inconceivable that the same land and the same language should continue all round the world ? I

[1] The best way is to imagine yourself walking round with the sun and asking the inhabitants as you go " what morning is this ? " if you suppose them living all the way round, and all speaking one language, the difficulty is obvious.

31

cannot see that it is : in that case either [1] there would
be no distinction at all between each successive day,
and so week, month &cc so that we should have to say
"the Battle of Waterloo happened to-day, about two
million hours ago," or some line would have to be
fixed, where the change should take place, so that the
inhabitant of one house would wake and say "heigh
ho ! [2] Tuesday morning ! " and the inhabitant of the
next, (over the line,) a few miles to the west would wake
a few minutes afterwards and say "heigh ho !
Wednesday morning ! " What hopeless confusion the
people who happened to live *on* the line would always
be in, it is not for me to say. There would be a quarrel
every morning as to what the name of the day should
be. I can imagine no third case, unless everybody
was allowed to choose for themselves, which state
of things would be rather worse than either of the
other two.

I am aware that this idea has been started before,
namely by the unknown author of that beautiful poem
beginning "If all the world were apple pie &cc." [3]

[1] This is clearly an impossible case, and is only put as an hypo-
thesis.

[2] The usual exclamation at waking : generally said with a yawn.

[3] "If all the world were apple pie,
    And all the sea were ink,
    And all the trees were bread and cheese,
    What *should* we have to drink ? "

The particular result here discussed however does not appear to have occurred to him, as he confines himself to the difficulties in obtaining drink which would certainly ensue.

Any good solution of the above difficulty will be thankfully received and inserted.

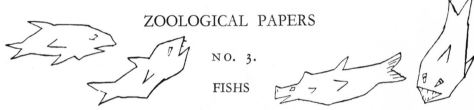

ZOOLOGICAL PAPERS

NO. 3.

FISHS

THE facts we have collected about this strange race of creatures are drawn partly from observation, partly from the works of a German author, whose name has not been given to the world. We believe that they [1] are only to be found in Germany : our author tells us they have " ordinarely [2] angles [3] at them," by which they " can be fanged, and heaved out of the water." The specimens which fell under our observation had *not* angles, as will shortly be seen, and therefore this sketch [4] is founded on mere conjecture.

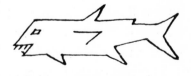

[1] i.e. Fishs. [2] As he spells it. [3] Or corners.
[4] The " angles " however may be supposed to be correct.

What the " fanging " consists of we cannot exactly say : if it is anything like a dog " fanging " a bone, it is certainly a strange mode of capture, but perhaps the writer refers to otters. The " heaving out of the water " we have likewise attempted to pourtray, though

here again fancy is our only guide. The reader probably will ask, " why put a *Crane* into the picture ? " our answer is " the only ' heaving ' we ever saw done was by means of a Crane."

This part of the subject however will be more properly treated of in the next paper.[1] Another fact our author

[1] Vide page 46.

gives us is that " they will very readily swim [1] after the pleasing direction of the staff " : this is easier to understand, as the simplest reader at once perceives that the only " staff " answering to this description is a stick of barley sugar. [2]

We will now attempt to describe the " fishs " which we examined. Skin hard and metallic ; colour brilliant, and of many hues ; body hollow ; (surprising  as this fact may appear, it is *perfectly true*) ; eyes large and meaningless ; fins fixed, and perfectly useless. They are wonderfully light, and have a sort of beak or snout of a metallic substance : as this is solid, and they have no other mouth, their hollowness is thus easily accounted for. The colour is sticky and comes off on the fingers, and they can swim back downwards just as easily as in the usual way. All these facts prove that they must not on any account be confounded with the English " fishes," which the similarity of names might at first lead us to do. They are a peculiar race of animals,[3] and must be treated as such. Our next subject [4] will be " The One-winged Dove."

[1] " Float " would be a better word, as their fins are immoveable.
[2] There is an objection to this solution, as " fishs " have no mouth.
[3] An incorrect expression : " creatures " would be better.
[4] Vide page 46.

LAYS OF SORROW

NO. I.

THE day was wet, the rain fell souse
　　Like jars of strawberry jam,[1] a
Sound was heard in the old hen-house,
　　A beating of a hammer.
Of stalwart form, and visage warm,
　　Two youths were seen within it,
Splitting up an old tree into perches for
　　　their poultry
　　At a hundred strokes[2] a minute.

The work is done, the hen has taken
Possession of her nest and eggs,
Without a thought of eggs and bacon,[3]
(Or I am very much mistaken :)
　　　She turns over each shell,
　　　To be sure that all's well,
　　　Looks into the straw
　　　To see there's no flaw,
　　　Goes once round the house,[4]
　　　Half afraid of a mouse,
　　　Then sinks calmly to rest
　　　On the top of her nest,
First doubling up each of her legs.

　　[1] i.e. the jam without the jars : observe the
beauty of this rhyme.
　　[2] At the rate of a stroke and two
thirds in a second.
　　[3] Unless the hen was a poacher,
which is unlikely.　[4] The hen-house.

Time rolled away, and so did every shell,
  "Small by degrees and beautifully less,"
As the sage mother with a powerful spell [1]
  Forced each in turn its contents to "express," [2]
    But ah! "imperfect is expression,"
    Some poet said, I don't care who,
    If you want to know you must go elsewhere,
    One fact I can tell, if you're willing to hear,
    He never attended a Parliament Session,
    For I'm certain that if he had ever been there,
    Full quickly would he have changed his ideas,
    With the hissings, the hootings, the groans and
      the cheers,
    And as to his name it is pretty clear
    That it wasn't me and it wasn't you!

And so it fell upon a day,
  (That is, it never rose again,)
A chick was found upon the hay,
Its little life had ebbed away,
No longer frolicsome and gay,
No longer could it run or play,
"And must we, chicken, must we part?"
Its master [3] cried with bursting heart,
  And voice of agony and pain.
So one, whose ticket's marked "Return," [4]

[1] Beak and claw.   [2] Press out.
[3] Probably one of the two stalwart youths.
[4] The system of return tickets is an excellent one. People are
conveyed, on particular days, there and back again for one fare.

When to the lonely roadside station
He flies in fear and perturbation,
Thinks of his home—the hissing urn—
Then runs with flying hat and hair,
And, entering, finds to his despair
  He's missed the very latest train! [1]

Too long it were to tell of each conjecture
  Of chicken suicide, and poultry victim,
The deadly frown, the stern and dreary lecture,
  The timid guess, "perhaps some needle pricked
    him!"
The din of voice, the words both loud and many,
  The sob, the tear, the sigh that none could smother,
Till all agreed: "a shilling to a penny
  It killed it self, and we acquit the mother!"
    Scarce was the verdict spoken,
    When that still calm was broken,
  A childish form hath burst into the throng,
    With tears and looks of sadness,
    That bring no news of gladness,
  But tell too surely something hath gone wrong!
  "The sight that I have come upon
    The stoutest [2] heart would sicken,
  That nasty hen has been and gone
    And killed another chicken!"

(*Continued page* 6o.)

[1] An additional vexation would be that his "Return" ticket
would be no use the next day.
[2] Perhaps even the "bursting" heart of its master.

SIR A. W. CALCOTT PAINTER.

J. C. BENTLEY ENGRAVER.

THE WOODEN BRIDGE.

from the picture in the Vernon Gallery.

THE VERNON GALLERY

" THE WOODEN BRIDGE "

A very few words will suffice to explain the meaning of this charming picture. Four ploughboys are trying to force an obstinate pig across a wooden bridge : the hands of a fifth are just visible at the edge of the picture. It appears either the height of cruelty or insanity to expect it to walk[1] across on one leg. This however they do not seem to have sufficiently considered, and the consequence is they are taking a great deal of trouble with scarcely a hope of success. It is scarcely possible for the unhappy creature to stand, much less to progress a single inch, until one or more of its legs are released. The fourth figure appears as if he would prefer no help at all in pulling to the help he is receiving.[2] The one who is pushing is evidently much of the same opinion. The trees, the cottage, and the setting sun in the background produce a fine effect.

[1] The word " walk " implies the use of more legs than one. The only way it could possibly advance would be hopping.
[2] Viz. by the hair.

THE WALKING-STICK OF DESTINY
Ch. 5.

READER! dare you enter once more the cave of the great Magician? If your heart be not bold, abstain: close these pages: read no more. High in air suspended hung the withered forms of two black cats; between was an owl, resting on a self-supported hideous viper.

The spiders were crawling on the long grey hair of the great Astrologer, as he wrote with letters of gold an awful spell on the magic scroll which hung from the deadly viper's mouth. A strange figure potatoe with over the mystic to be reading side down. like an animated[1] arms and legs hovered scroll, and appeared the words up- Hark!

A shrill scream rolled round the cave, echoing from

---

[1] It had a "hollow" voice and probably was something akin to "fishs"; vide page 35.

41

side to side till it died[1] away in the massive roof.
Horror! yet did not the Magician's heart quail, albeit
his little finger shook slightly thrice, and one of his few
grey hairs stood out straight from his head, erect with
terror: there was one other that would have followed
its example, but a spider was hanging on it, and it
could not.

A flash of mystic light, black[2] as the darkest ebony,
now pervades the place, and in its momentary gleam
the owl is seen to wink once. Dread omen! Did its
supporting viper hiss? Ah no! that would be *too*
terrible! In the deep dead silence which followed this
thrilling event, a solitary sneeze was distinctly heard
from the left-hand cat. Distinct, and now the Magician
did tremble. "Gloomy spirits of the vasty deep!"
he murmured in faltering tone, as his aged limbs seemed
about to sink beneath him, "I did not call for ye: why
come ye?" He spoke, and the potatoe answered, in
hollow tone: "Thou didst!" then all was silence.

The magician recoiled in terror. What! bearded[3]
by a potatoe![4] never! He smote his aged breast in

---

[1] After its death its ghost appeared; page 43.

[2] It is difficult to imagine what black light can look like. It
may be obtained by pouring ink over a candle in a dark room.

[3] Vide page 10.

[4] The potatoe's history should be carefully remembered, as it
is important.

anguish, and then collecting strength to speak, he shouted, "Speak but the word again, and on the spot I'll boil thee!" There was an ominous pause, long, vague, and mysterious. What is about to happen? The potatoe sobbed audibly, and its thick showering tears were heard falling heavily down on the rocky floor. Then slow, clear, and terrible came the awful words: "Gobno strodgol slok slabolgo!"[1] and then in a low hissing whisper "'tis time!"

"Mystery! mystery!" groaned the horrified Astrologer, "The Russian war cry! oh Slogdod! Slogdod! what hast thou done?" He stood expectant, tremulous; but no sound met his anxious ear; nothing but the ceaseless dribble of the far-off waterfall. At length a voice said "now!" and at the word the right-hand cat fell with a heavy thump to the earth. Then an Awful Form[2] was seen, dimly looming through the darkness: it prepared to speak, but a universal cry[3] of "corkscrews!" resounded through the cave, and with a noiseless howl it vanished. A rapid fluttering was now heard pervading the whole cave, three[4] voices cried "yes!" at the same moment, and it was light.

[1] This is quoted from *Punch*: it is there stated that after singing this the soldiers are never known to give or receive quarter.

[2] The ghost of the shrill scream; vide page 41.

[3] It rolled spirally round the cave.

[4] The Awful Form, the potatoe, and the right-hand cat.

Dazzling light, so that the Magician shuddering closed his eyes, and said, " It is a dream, oh that I could wake ! " He looked up, and cave, Form, cats, everything were gone : nothing remained before him but the magic scroll and pen, a stick of red sealing wax, and a lighted wax taper.

" August potatoe ! " he muttered," I obey your potent voice." Then sealing up the mystic roll, he summoned a courier, and dispatched it : " Haste for thy life, post ! haste ! haste ! for thy life post ! haste ! " were the last words the frightened man heard dinned in his ears as he gallopped off.

Then with a heavy sigh the great magician turned back into the gloomy cave, murmuring in a hollow tone, Now for the toad ! " [1]

(*Continued page* 56.)

[1] Vide page 59. The toad was always necessary to magical rites, see Shakespeare's " Macbeth."

REPRESENTATIVE MEN [1]

LECTURE 1st

"ON THE USES OF LITTLE MEN"

" THE world is made of little men." 'Tis a little saying, but how true! Go where you will, you meet them: they are the majority of the people, the nobility, the army, the orators. Can an army exist without private soldiers? no more than a house without bricks. For every great man, there are 10,000 little men : aye, and there is work for them, which no great man would do. Do not little men build our houses and ships, till our land, and supply our various wants? Ask the great Alexander to make a pudding. Faugh! But the pudding *must* be made. A most important class truly! and all-worthy of a representative. How profoundly little was the saying of the countryman [2] when the dumplings came to table, " Them's the jockeys for my money ! "

The great men round him laughed at it ; *we* know its value. Look at *The Times* : " the smallest terrier in England, lowest price £25." Little ! little ! is still the cry. Draw up the curtain ! Enter, little man !

(*Continued page* 55.)

[1] After " Emerson's Representative Men."
[2] A well-known anecdote.

45

ZOOLOGICAL PAPERS

NO. 4.

THE ONE-WINGED DOVE

ALL the information we can collect on this subject is taken from an advertisement in *The Times*, July 2, 1850, the rest is conjecture.

To begin with the advertisement, " The One-winged Dove must Die, unless the Crane returns to be a shield against her enemies." From this we draw the following facts. (1) It is a dove with one wing. (2) The Crane is its friend. (3) It has enemies who wish its death. (4) The Crane alone can resist these enemies. (5) The Crane has left it. (6) (from the mere fact of the advertisement being sent to *The Times*) The Dove can write. (7) (from the same fact) The Crane can read. (8) (do.) The Dove has more than 12*s*. in the world. (9) (do.) The Crane takes in *The Times*.

So that here is at any rate a reasonable foundation for conjecture. You are not so clever [1] as we are, Reader, so it will not be surprising if you have not yet discovered that facts (1) and (6) are connected together,[2] and

---

[1] This is not meant to disparage the mental capacities of readers in general, or of any reader in particular. Who knows but that Faraday himself may read these pages ? Yet, considering the transcendent intellects of the Editor, this assertion, in any given case, has every probability of being true. [2] Vide page 49.

explain each other. Have you now? confess! There is another discovery which has probably hitherto escaped your notice, namely, that facts (2) and (3) are similarly connected.[1] So now to begin.[2]

The Crane and the Dove are friends.[3] This is natural, as they are both birds: it seems hardly necessary to speculate on the origin of this friendship, perhaps their mutual talents,[4] namely, reading and writing, first led to it.

The Dove has but one wing,[5] that is, it has lost the other. This is *un*natural, but we hope to account for it soon. It is evidently this misfortune which prevents its escaping from its enemies,[6] and this gives us the first clue as to the nature of those enemies. Clearly they cannot be birds; two wings would be no protection against *them*: neither can they be beasts,[7] against whom the Crane could be no protection[8]: they are as clearly not English; the Crane is not wild in England[9]: insects are too contemptible a foe. There is only one

[1] Vide page 49.

[2] Not that we have not begun already, but here commences that close, learned, and unanswerable argument which has made this paper so deservedly celebrated.

[3] Fact (2).

[4] Or "accomplishments," which, though common among men, are rarely found in other creatures.

[5] Fact (1).   [6] Fact (3).   [7] Or quadrupeds.   [8] Fact (4).

[9] See Buffon: "wild" does not here mean "savage" but "undomesticated."

thing left : come, Reader ! you shall have the credit of guessing ! that's right ! " Fishs." Not " fishes," mind ! *that* is an English name, but " fishs."

And we are here met by a startling, a thrilling confirmation in the fact that a *Crane* is to be the shield against these enemies. Turn back, Reader, to the paper[1] on " Fishs " : what is employed to " fang " those " fishs ? " to " heave them out of the water," and so to destroy them ? is it not a Crane ? This conclusion, then, cannot be disputed.

" Fishs," then, are the Dove's enemies. But why ? what occasioned this enmity ? everything must have a reason. Be patient, Reader. The Dove, we know, is talented[2] : it therefore probably writes in *Punch* : " fishs " have " angles " : " angle " is a word of two meanings. What so natural, then, as that it should write jokes on " fishs " ? This would of course enrage the said " fishs," and enmity would thereby arise. Is not this clear enough ? We know also that " fishs " were long ere this enemies to the Crane, because of its habit of " fanging " them, and " heaving them out of the water." The Crane then was, of all birds, the most proper friend for the Dove to appeal to.

" But," say you, " how could ' fishs ' kill the Dove ? "

[1] Page 33.

[2] The use of this word is explained in the preceding page : note (4).

Oh most stupid and ignorant Reader! have not "fishs" got "angles"? are not "angles" sharp and jagged? How easy then with them to kill so tender [1] a creature as a One-Winged Dove! And now for the grand question, "how did the Dove lose it's wing?" and the mysterious connection between facts (1) and (6). Reader! you shall guess again. The Dove writes in *Punch* [2] : pens are used in writing : pens are procured from feathers [3] : feathers from—yes! you're right! "it uses its own feathers." Perhaps you are not aware that *Punch* has been in existence nine years, so that if the Dove was a contributor from the first, the loss of one whole wing is thus easily accounted for. You will surely allow that thus far at least, we build our conjectures entirely on fact?

Is it likely that the Crane should have left the Dove [4] in its present defenceless condition? Certainly not. [5] We may safely conclude that it left it while still able to defend itself. When was that? Calculate for yourself, Reader. *Punch* comes out once a week : probably

[1] By this is not meant that it is tenderer than other doves.

[2] See preceding page.

[3] Generally of a goose or swan, but there is no reason why a Dove's should not be used.

[4] Fact (5).

[5] If the Dove was tender-bodied, we may safely conclude that the Crane was tender-hearted, and would "heave" a sigh at the misfortunes of others.

49

the Dove writes one article in each number,[1] that is, uses one pen or feather each week : thirteen feathers would probably [2] make a wing large enough to fly with : it has evidently *none* now : thirteen weeks from the date of its first advertisement brings us to April 7 : can't you guess now ? Well then, we must tell you. On April 7th a great *Protectionist* Meeting took place in London. Still stupid ? Reader ! you are wonderfully slow of comprehension ! does not the Crane *protect* the Dove ? what other motive *could* it have then for going up to London on the 7th but attending that meeting ?

And now what conclusion are we to draw from the facts that the Dove has more than 12*s*.,[3] and that the Crane takes in *The Times* [4] ? We may as well just mention that 12*s*. is the usual price [5] for inserting such an advertisement in a newspaper. Simply this. The Dove is rich [6] : therefore it pays the Crane for defending it, and this accounts for the Crane's taking in *The Times* : where else could it get the money to do so ? " But

[1] That is, every Thursday. The Umbrella comes out every rainy day.

[2] This cannot be known for certain without making the experiment.

[3] Fact (8).　　　　　　　　　[4] Fact (9).

[5] We believe the charge is five shillings a line : an advertisement lately inserted, which took up a whole page cost three hundred pounds.

[6] This is further seen from the fact that this advertisement was put in three or four days running.

where," you ask, "where does the Dove get *its* money?" That, gentle Reader, is its own affair. We know that it *has* money because otherwise it could not advertise.

One question yet remains unanswered; "where does the Dove live?" that is easily disposed of. "Fishs" are only found in Germany. *There* then the Dove lives. As evidently the Crane is in England, else why advertise[1] for it in an English paper? "But it left Germany thirteen weeks ago!" you say, "cruel Crane! why does it not return?" Reader, we echo the question, and we tremble as we do so. The life of a Crane in England is no safe or easy life: even at this moment probably the Crane is either dead or in a cage. This alone can account for its silence. Alas! poor Dove![2] what will you do? you state yourself that you "must die." We fear it is only too true.

We are aware that one objection can be brought against this argument, namely, that no one remembers seeing any jokes in *Punch* about "Fishs." This however is no real argument, as the statement at best is negative, and besides, how faithless a thing is memory!

[1] How the Dove being abroad, could advertise in England, we confess we cannot explain.

[2] Shakespeare's "Alas, poor Yorick!" though inferior to this passage in simplicity, is almost equal to it in poetical pathos. It seems hardly necessary to add that the idea was *originated* by the Editor, who would scorn to copy any author.

Will you, oh Reader, be certain you can remember every joke *Punch* has published for nine years ?

We have dwelt thus long and earnestly on this subject, as knowing its difficulty and importance : still we hope we have established *some* facts, cleared up *some* doubts, solved *some* difficulties. At all events we have done our best : we cannot name any subject for our next paper, nor are we at all sure there will be another at all, so at any rate for the present, good Reader, farewell !

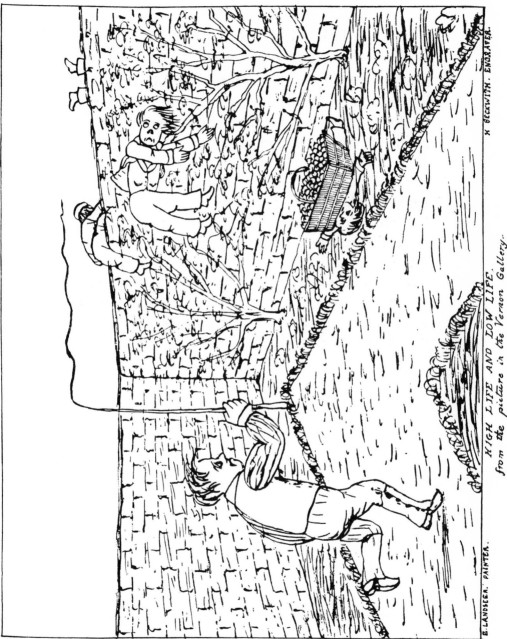

E. LANDSEER, PAINTER.

HIGH LIFE AND LOW LIFE.
from the picture in the Vernon Gallery.

H BECKWITH, ENGRAVER.

THE VERNON GALLERY
"HIGH LIFE AND LOW LIFE"

NEVER was the name of a picture more fully borne out in the picture than in this. The face of the boy suspended on the wall, representing "High Life," is positively exquisite [1] : we have rarely seen anything more true to nature. One can trace in it, besides fear of the approaching gardener, a shade of sorrow and regret for the basket of apples [2] he has just dropped. His companion however, whose face is just visible from under the basket, probably feels more *real* sorrow for that event. This last, the reader will of course perceive, is meant to represent "Low Life." The gardener is admirably drawn, but the potatoe beds and gravel walk are rather inferior to the artist's usual style. On the whole, however, the picture does him great credit.

[1] i.e. expressing exquisite pain.   [2] Probably Lemon Pippins.

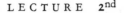

REPRESENTATIVE MEN

LECTURE 2nd

"CUFFEY, OR THE CHARTIST"

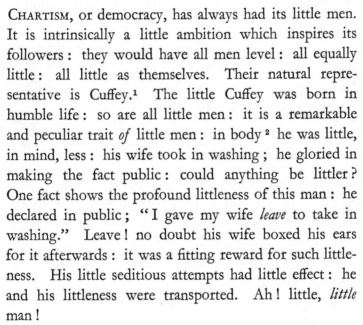

CHARTISM, or democracy, has always had its little men. It is intrinsically a little ambition which inspires its followers : they would have all men level : all equally little : all little as themselves. Their natural representative is Cuffey.[1] The little Cuffey was born in humble life : so are all little men : it is a remarkable and peculiar trait *of* little men : in body [2] he was little, in mind, less : his wife took in washing ; he gloried in making the fact public : could anything be littler ? One fact shows the profound littleness of this man : he declared in public ; " I gave my wife *leave* to take in washing." Leave ! no doubt his wife boxed his ears for it afterwards : it was a fitting reward for such littleness. His little seditious attempts had little effect : he and his littleness were transported. Ah ! little, *little* man !

(Continued at page 66.)

[1] The history of this man may be found in *The Times*.
[2] He was a tailor and therefore only the ninth part of a man, as every one knows.

THE WALKING-STICK OF DESTINY
Ch. 6.

HUSH! The Baron slumbers! two men with stealthy steps are removing his strong-box.[1] It is very heavy, and their knees tremble, partly with the weight, partly with fear. He snores and they both

start: the box rattles, not a moment is to be lost, they hasten from the room. It was very, very hard to get the box out of the window but they did it at last, though not without making noise enough to waken ten ordinary sleepers: the Baron, luckily for them, was an *extra-* ordinary sleeper.

At a safe distance from the castle they set down the box, and proceeded to force off the lid. Four mortal hours[2] did Mr. Milton Smith and his mysterious companion labour thereat: at sunrise it flew off with a

[1] Its contents, as afterwards appears were very small; vide page 27, note (1).

[2] Probably they began at about one o'clock.

56

noise louder than the explosion of fifty powder-mag-azines,[1] which was heard for miles and miles around. The Baron sprang from his couch at the sound, and full furiously did he ring his bell : up rushed the terrified domestic, and tremblingly related when he got down stairs again, how " his Honour was wisibly flustrated, and pitched the poker [2] at him more than ordinary savage-like ! " But to return to our two adventurers : as soon as they recovered from the swoon into which the explosion had thrown them, they proceeded to examine the contents of the box. Mr. M. Smith timidly put his head into it, his companion still remaining stretched on the ground, and being too lazy to get up.

There was a minute's pause, and then Mr. M. Smith drew a long breath, and ejaculated, " Well ! I never ! " " Well ! you never ! " angrily repeated the other, " what's the good of going on like that ? just tell us what's in the box, and don't make such an ass of yourself ! " " My dear fellow ! " interposed the poet, " I give you my honour—" " I wouldn't give twopence [3] for your honour," retorted his friend, savagely tearing up the grass by handfuls, " give me what's in the box, that's a

[1] The amount of this noise can only be guessed at, as the experiment has never been tried.

[2] Probably red hot ; vide page 16.

[3] We may therefore conclude it to have been worth about three-half-pence, " honour among thieves " is a proverbial expression, so they most likely had about three-pennyworth between them.

deal more valuable." "Well but you won't hear me
out, I was just going to tell you; there's nothing whatever in the box but a walking-stick! and that's a fact;
if you won't believe me, come and look yourself!"
"You don't say so!" shouted his companion, springing
to his feet, his laziness gone in a moment, "sure*ly* there's
more than that!" "I tell you there isn't!" replied the
poet rather sulkily, as he stretched himself on the grass.

The other one however turned the box over, and
examined it on all sides before he would be convinced,
and then carelessly twirling the stick on his forefinger
he began: "I suppose it's no use taking *this* to Baron
Muggzwig? it'll be no sort of use." "Well, I don't
know!" was the somewhat hesitating reply, "it might
be as well—you see he didn't say what he expected—"
"*I* know that, you donkey!" interrupted the other
impatiently, "but I don't suppose he expected a walking-
stick! if that had been all, do you think he'd have given
us ten dollars a piece to do the job?" "I'm sure I
can't say," muttered the poet: "Well! do as you please
then!" said his companion angrily, and flinging the
walking-stick at him as he spoke he walked hastily away.

Never had he of the hat and cloak thrown away such
a good opportunity of making his fortune! At twelve [1]
o'clock that day a visitor was announced to Baron

[1] So that it was a 7-hours' walk from Baron Slogdod's to Baron
Muggzwig's.

Muggzwig, and our poet entering placed the walking-stick in his hands. The Baron's eyes flashed with joy, and hastily placing a large purse of gold in his hand he said, " Adieu for the present, my dear friend ! you shall hear from me again ! " and then he carefully locked up the stick muttering, " nothing is now wanting but the toad ! "

LAYS OF SORROW

NO. 2.

FAIR stands the ancient[1] Rectory,
  The Rectory of Croft,
The sun shines bright upon it,
  The breezes whisper soft.
From all the house and garden
  Its inhabitants come forth,
And muster in the road without,
And pace in twos and threes about,
  The children of the North.

Some are waiting in the garden,
  Some are waiting at the door,
And some are following behind,
  And some have gone before.
But wherefore all this mustering?
  Wherefore this vast array?
A gallant feat of horsemanship
  Will be performed today.

[1] This Rectory has been supposed to have been built in the time of Edward the sixth, but recent discoveries clearly assign its origin to a much earlier period. A stone has been found in an island formed by the river Tees, on which is inscribed the letter " A," which is justly conjectured to stand for the name of the great king Alfred, in whose reign this house was probably built.

To eastward and to westward,
  The crowd divides amain,
Two youths are leading on the steed,
  Both tugging at the rein:
And sorely do they labour,
  For the steed [1] is very strong,
And backward moves its stubborn feet,
And backward ever doth retreat,
  And drags its guides along.

And now the knight hath mounted,
  Before the admiring band,
Hath got the stirrups on his feet,
  The bridle in his hand.
Yet, oh! beware, sir horseman!
  And tempt thy fate no more,
For such a steed as thou hast got,
  Was never rid before!

The rabbits [2] bow before thee,
  And cower in the straw;
The chickens [3] are submissive,
  And own thy will for law;

[1] The poet entreats pardon for having represented a donkey under this dignified name.

[2] With reference to these remarkable animals see "Moans from the Miserable," page 12.

[3] A full account of the history and misfortunes of these interesting creatures may be found in the first "Lay of Sorrow," page 36.

Bullfinches and canary
   Thy bidding do obey;
And e'en the tortoise in its shell
   Doth never say thee nay.

But thy steed will hear no master,
   Thy steed will bear no stick,
And woe to those that beat her,
   And woe to those that kick [1] !
For though her rider smite her,
   As hard as he can hit,
And strive to turn her from the yard,
She stands in silence, pulling hard
   Against the pulling bit.

And now the road to Dalton
   Hath felt their coming tread,
The crowd are speeding on before,
   And all have gone ahead.
Yet often look they backward,
   And cheer him on, and bawl,
For slower still and still more slow,
That horseman and that charger go,
   And scarce advance at all.

[1] It is a singular fact that a donkey makes a point of returning
any kicks offered to it.

And now two roads to choose from
  Are in that rider's sight :
In front, the road to Dalton,
  And New Croft upon the right.
" I can't get by ! " he bellows,
  " I really am not able !
Though I pull my shoulder out of joint,
  I cannot get him past this point,
For it leads unto his stable ! "

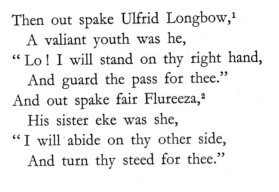

Then out spake Ulfrid Longbow,[1]
  A valiant youth was he,
" Lo ! I will stand on thy right hand,
  And guard the pass for thee."
And out spake fair Flureeza,[2]
  His sister eke was she,
" I will abide on thy other side,
  And turn thy steed for thee."

And now commenced a struggle
  Between that steed and rider,
For all the strength that he hath left,
  Doth not suffice to guide her.

---

[1] This valiant knight besides having a heart of steel, and nerves
of iron, has been lately in the habit of carrying a brick in his eye.
[2] She was sister to both.

63

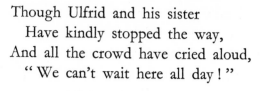

Though Ulfrid and his sister
  Have kindly stopped the way,
And all the crowd have cried aloud,
  " We can't wait here all day ! "

Round turned he, as not deigning
  Their words to understand,
But he slipped the stirrups from his feet,
  The bridle from his hand.
And grasped the mane full lightly,
  And vaulted from his seat,
And gained the road in triumph,[1]
  And stood upon his feet.

All firmly till that moment
  Had Ulfrid Longbow stood,
And faced the foe right valiantly,
  As every warrior should.
But when safe on terra firma
  His brother he did spy,
" What *did* you do that for ? " he cried,
Then unconcerned he stepped aside,
  And let it canter by.

[1] The reader will probably be at a loss to discover the nature
of this triumph, as no object was gained, and the donkey was
obviously the victor, on this point however, we are sorry to say,
we can offer no good explanation.

64

They gave him bread and butter,[1]
  That was of public right,
As much as four strong rabbits,
  Could munch from morn to night.
For he'd done a deed of daring,
  And faced that savage steed,
And therefore cups of coffee sweet,
And everything that was a treat,
  Were but his right and meed.

And often in the evenings,
  When the fire is blazing bright,
When books bestrew the table,
  And moths obscure the light,
When crying children go to bed,
  A struggling, kicking load,
We'll talk of Ulfrid Longbow's deed,
How, in his brother's utmost need,
Back to his aid he flew with speed,
And how he faced the fiery steed,
  And kept the New Croft Road.

[1] Much more acceptable to a true knight than " cornland " which the Roman people were so foolish as to give to their daring champion, Horatius.

REPRESENTATIVE MEN

LECTURE 3d.

"JACK SPRAT, OR THE EPICURE"

WE have the highest authority for stating the fact that Jack, or John Sprat[1] could eat no fat. The conviction bursts upon us with such a blaze of evidence, that room for doubt there is none. Now, even if we grant that he had a "little" appetite, and so was not sufficiently hungry to desire to eat fat—even granting this, I say, and the admission, instead of lessening, would but strengthen my argument for the littleness of the man —still how can anyone pretend to set aside or step over the fact that he permitted his wife to refuse lean? Yes! it is so stated: "his wife would eat no lean": not a word is said of his putting a stop to her whims: no, he submitted with true littleness of mind. All epicures are little, and he is but a common specimen of the class.

[1] A shade of doubt has been cast over the authenticity of this anecdote on account of the rhyme between "Sprat" and "fat": a singular coincidence.

W. ETTY. R.A. PAINTER.   THE DUETT.   R. BELL. ENGRAVER.

from the picture in the Vernon Gallery.

THE VERNON GALLERY
" THE DUETT "

THIS charming picture is intended to represent three true lovers of music; for though the boy on the left is taking no part in the performance, yet there is a fire in his eye which forbids us to think him an inattentive or unadmiring listener. The most casual observer cannot fail to remark what a tendency the love of music has to make the hair grow in full luxuriance, nay, he may safely conclude, if he finds no such effect produced in *him*, that he has no ear for melody. A further proof of the lady's great musical taste is that she is producing the most mellow strains from a pair of common kitchen bellows [1] : the song they are singing my readers have no doubt often heard.

[1] This, in point of fact, is the only instrument by means of which a brisk air can be produced. It's use requires a strict attention to the bars.

THE WALKING-STICK OF DESTINY
Ch. 7.

THE Baron Muggzwig was fat.[1] Far be it from the humble author of these pages to insinuate that his fatness exceeded the bounds of proportion, or the manly beauty of the human figure, but he certainly was fat, and of that fact there is not the shadow of a doubt. It may perhaps have been owing to this fatness of body that a certain thickness and obtuseness of intellect was at times perceptible in the noble Baron. In his ordinary conversation he was, to say the least of it, misty and obscure, but after dinner or when at all excited his language certainly verged on the incomprehensible. This was perhaps owing to his liberal use of the parenthesis without any definite pause to mark the different clauses of the sentence. He used to consider his arguments unanswer-

[1] This Laconic commencement bears some resemblance to Hood's " My aunt Shakerly was of enormous bulk," in his " Whims and Oddities." It his hardly necessary to state which was the original.

able, and they certainly were so perplexing, and generally reduced his hearers to such a state of bewilderment and stupefaction, that few ever ventured to attempt an answer to them.

He usually however compensated [1] in length for what his speeches wanted in clearness, and it was owing to this cause that his visitors, on the morning we are speaking of had to blow the trumpet at the gate three times before they were admitted, as the footman was at that moment undergoing a lecture from his master, supposed to have reference to the yesterday's dinner, but which, owing to a slight admixture of extraneous matter in the discourse, left on the footman's mind a confused impression that his master had been partly scolding him for not keeping a stricter watch on the fishing trade, partly setting forth his own private views on the management of railway shares, and partly finding fault with the bad arrangement of financial affairs [2] in the moon.

In this state of mind it is not surprising that his first

[1] The author must be understood to say that length *is* any compensation for clearness, though there certainly have been orators who seem to have held that opinion.

[2] Our range of information on this subject is extremely limited. There would appear to be an over-hasty precipitation in the conduct of its inhabitant, who is related to have " come down too soon."

answer to their question, "Is the Baron at home?" should be, "The fish, sir, was the cook's affair, I had nothing whatsumdever to do with it," which on reflection he immediately afterwards corrected to, "the trains was late, so it was unpossible as the wine could come sooner." "The man is surely mad or drunk!" angrily exclaimed one of the strangers, no other than the mysterious man in a cloak: "Not so," was the reply

in gentle voice, as the great magician stepped forward, "but let me interrogate him—ho! fellow!" he continued in a louder tone, "is thy master at home?" The man gazed at him for a moment like one in a dream, and then suddenly recollecting himself he replied, "I begs pardon, gentlemen, the Baron *is* at home: would you please to walk in?" and with these words he ushered them up stairs.

On entering the room they made a low obeisance,

and the Baron starting from his seat exclaimed with singular rapidity, " And even if you have called on behalf of Slogdod that infatuated wretch and I'm sure I've often told him—" " We have called," gravely interrupted the Magician, " to ascertain whether—" " Yes," continued the excited [1] Baron, " scores of times aye scores of times I have and you may believe me or not as you like for though—" " To ascertain," persisted the Magician, " whether you have in your possession,[2] and if so—" " But yet " broke in Muggzwig, " he always would and as he used to say if—" " And if so," shouted the man in a cloak despairing of the Magician ever getting through the sentence, " to know what you would like to be done with regard to Signor Blowski." So saying, they retired a few steps, and waited for the Baron's reply, and their host, without further delay delivered the following remarkable [3] speech : " And though I have no wish to provoke the

[1] Wherefore excited ? the thoughtful reader will doubtless inquire. The only circumstance we can offer in explanation is his recent squabble with the footman.

[2] Understand " the Walking-stick of Destiny."

[3] It is hoped that a ready solution of any little difficulties and inconsistences which may have occurred in the course of the story will be found by the attentive reader, in this speech, no less remarkable for its rapid change of subject, than for its uninterrupted flow.

enmity which considering the provocations I have received and really if you reckon them up they are more than any mortal man let alone a Baron for the family temper has been known for years to be beyond  nay the royal family themselves will hardly boast of considering too that he has so long a time kept which I shouldn't have found out only that rascal Blowski said and how he could bring himself to tell all those lies I can't think for I always considered him quite honest and of course wishing if possible to prove him innocent [1] and the walking-stick since it is absolutely necessary in such matters and begging your pardon I consider the toad and all that humbug but that's between you and me and even when I had sent for it by two of my bandits [2] and one of them bringing it to me yesterday for which I gave him a purse of gold and I hope he was grateful for it and though the employment of bandits

---

[1] The reader will naturally ask in what his guilt consisted, and for an answer we can only refer him to the first chapter.

[2] This explains who the man in the cloak was.

is at all times and particularly in this case if you consider
the but even on account of some civilities he showed
me though I daresay there was something and by-the-
bye perhaps that was the reason he pitched himself I
mean him out of the window for—" here he paused,
seeing that his visitors in despair had left the room.
Now, Reader, prepare yourself for the last chapter.

THE WALKING-STICK OF DESTINY

Ch. 8 AND LAST

ALL was silence.[1] The Baron Slogdod was seated in the hall of his ancestors, in his chair of state, but his countenance wore not its usual expression of calm content: there was an uncomfortable restlessness about him which betokened a mind ill at ease, for why? closely packed in the hall around, so densely wedged together as to resemble one vast living ocean without a gap or hollow, were seated seven thousand human beings: all eyes were bent upon him, each breath was held in eager expectation, and he felt, he felt in his inmost heart, though he vainly endeavoured to conceal his uneasiness under a forced and unnatural smile, that something awful was about to happen. Reader! if your nerves are not adamant, turn not this page!

Before the Baron's seat there stood a table: what sat thereon? well knew the trembling crowds, as with blanched cheek and tottering knees they gazed upon it, and shrank from it even while they gazed: ugly, deformed, ghastly and hideous it sat, with large dull eyes, and bloated cheeks, the magic toad!

[1] This chapter, it is hoped, will clear up all the mystery in the story.

75

All feared and loathed it, save the Baron only, who, rousing himself at intervals from his gloomy meditations, would raise his toe, and give it a sportive[1] kick, of which it took not the smallest notice. *He* feared it not, no, deeper terrors possessed *his* mind, and clouded his brow with anxious thought.

Beneath the table was crouched a quivering mass, so abject and grovelling as scarce to bear the form of humanity: none regarded, and none pitied it.

Then outspake the Magician: " The man I accuse,[2] if man indeed he be, is—Blowski ! " At the word, the shrunken form arose, and displayed to the horrified assemby the well-known vulture face : he opened his mouth to speak, but no sound issued from his pale and trembling lips . . . a solemn stillness settled on all around . . . the Magician raised the walking-stick of destiny, and in thrilling accents pronounced the fatal words : " Recreant vagabond ! misguided reprobrate ! receive thy due deserts ! " . . . Silently he sank to the earth . . . all was dark for a moment, . . . returning light revealed to their gaze . . . a heap of mashed

[1] Sportive in fact only, but the gloomy mind of the Baron was far from entertaining any sportive thoughts at that moment.

[2] It may well be asked " of what ? " and the author regrets he cannot furnish an answer.

potatoe[1] . . . a globular form faintly loomed through the darkness, and howled once audibly, then all was still. Reader, our tale is told.

[1] Many have vainly asked the author, " What had he done ? " He don't know.

DIFFICULTIES

N O. 2.

WHICH is the best, a clock that is right only once a year, or a clock that is right twice every day? " The latter," you reply, "unquestionably." Very good, reader, now attend.

I have two clocks: one doesn't go *at all*, and the other loses a minute a day: which would you prefer? " The losing one," you answer, " without a doubt." Now observe : the one which loses a minute a day has to lose twelve hours, or seven hundred and twenty minutes before it is right again, consequently it is only right once in two years, whereas the other is evidently right as often as the time it points to comes round, which happens twice a day. So you've contradicted yourself *once* : " Ah, but," you say, " what's the use of its being right twice a day, if I can't tell when the time comes ? " Why, suppose the clock points to eight o'clock, don't you see that the clock is right *at* eight o'clock ? Consequently when eight o'clock comes your clock is right. " Yes, I see *that*," you reply.[1]

[1] You *might* go on to ask, " How am I to know when eight o'clock *does* come ? my clock will not tell me." Be patient, reader : you know that when eight o'clock comes your clock is right : very good ; then your rule is this : keep your eye fixed on your clock, and *the very moment it is right* it will be eight o'clock. " But—" you say. There, that'll do, reader ; the more you argue, the farther you get from the point, so it will be as well to stop.

78

Very good, then you've contradicted yourself *twice* :
now get out of the difficulty as you can, and don't
contradict yourself again if you can help it.

THE POET'S FAREWELL

ALL day he had sat without a hat,
   The comical old feller,
Shading his form from the driving storm
   With the Rectory Umbrella.
When the storm had passed by, and the ground was dry,
   And the sun shon bright on the plain,
He arose from his seat, and he stood on his feet,
   And sang a melting strain :

      All is o'er ! the sun is setting,
         Soon will sound the dinner bell ;
      Thou hast saved me from a wetting,
         Here I'll take my last farewell !
      Far dost thou eclipse the Maga-
         zines which came before thy day,
      And thy coming made them stagger,
         Like the stars at morning ray.
      Let me call again their phantoms,
         And their voices long gone by,
      Like the crow of distant bantams,
         Or the buzzing of a fly.

First in age, but not in merit,
   Stands the Rectr'y Magazine;
All its wit thou dost inherit,
   Though the Comet came between.
Novelty was in its favour,
   And mellifluous its lays,
All, with eager plaudits, gave a
   Vote of honour in its praise.

Next in order comes the Comet,
   Like some vague and feverish dream,
Gladly, gladly turn I from it,
   To behold thy rising beam!
When I first began to edit,
   In the Rect'ry Magazine,
Each one wrote therein who read it,
   Each one read who wrote therein.
When the Comet next I started,
   They grew lazy as a drone:
Gradually all departed,
   Leaving me to write alone.
But in thee—let future ages
   Mark the fact which I record,
No one helped me in *thy* pages,
   Even with a single word!

But the wine has left the cellar,
   And I hear the dinner bell,
So fare thee well, my old Umbrella,
   Dear Umbrella, fare thee well!

THE INDEX

THE INDEX

Mischmasch

PREFACE

" YET once more," (to use the time-honoured words of our poet Milton,) we present ourselves before an eager and expectant public, let us hope under even better auspices than hitherto.

In making our bow for the—may we venture to say so ?—fourth time, it will be worth while to review the past, and to consider the probable future. We are encouraged to do so by Mrs. Malaprop's advice, " Let us not anticipate the past : let all our retrospections be to the future," and by the fact that our family motto is " Respiciendo prudens."

We purpose then to give a brief history of our former domestic magazines in this family, their origin, aim, progress, and ultimate fate, and we shall notice, as we go on, the other magazines which have appeared, but not under our own editorship : we commence our history, then, with

USEFUL AND INSTRUCTIVE POETRY

This we wrote ourselves about the year 1845, the idea of the first poem being suggested by a piece in the " Etonian " : it lasted about half a year, and was then very clumsily bound up in a sort of volume : the binding, however, was in every respect worthy of the contents : the volume still exists.

THE RECTORY MAGAZINE

This was the first started for general contribution, and at first the contributions poured in in one continuous stream, while the issuing of each number was attended by the most violent excitement through the whole house : most of the family contributed one or more articles to it. About the year 1848 the numbers were bound into a volume, which still exists.

THE COMET

This was started by us about the year 1848. It was the same shape as the former, but, for the sake of variety, opened at the end instead of the side. Little interest attended this publication, and its contents were so poor, that, after 6 numbers were out, we destroyed all but the last, and published no more. The last number, we believe, is still in existence.

THE ROSEBUD

This was started in imitation of the Comet, but only reached a second number : the cover of each number was tastefully ornamented with a painted rosebud : the two numbers do not contain much worth notice, but are still preserved.

THE STAR

Another imitator of the Comet, on a less ambitious scale even than the last : the manuscript and illustrations decidedly below par : some half-dozen numbers still survive.

THE WILL-O'-THE-WISP

Even inferior to the last : the numbers were cut in a triangular shape : we believe some numbers are still to be found.

THE RECTORY UMBRELLA

This we started, we believe, in 1849 or 1850, in a ready-bound square volume. It was admired at the time, but wholly unsupported, and it took us a year or more to fill the volume by our own unaided efforts. The volume exists, and in good preservation, and therefore any further account of it is needless.

We will here notice one or two of our own writings, which have seen more extended publicity than the above mentioned. In the summer of 1854 we contributed two poems to the "Oxonian Advertiser," neither at all worth preservation; and in the Long Vacation of the same year, when staying with a reading party at Whitby, we contributed "The Lady of the Ladle" and "Wilhelm von Schmitz," to the weekly Gazette of that place. Both will be found inserted in this volume. From this subject we hasten to the consideration of the present magazine.

MISCHMASCH

The name is German, and means in English "midge-madge," which we need not inform the intelligent reader is equivalent to "hodge-podge": our intention is to admit articles of every kind, prose, verse, and pictures, provided they reach a sufficiently high standard of merit.

The best of its contents will be offered at intervals to a contemporary magazine of a less exclusively domestic nature: we allude to the "Comic Times"; thus affording to the contributors to this magazine an opportunity of presenting their productions to the admiring gaze of the English Nation.

CROFT. *Aug*: 13. 1855.

"Be rather in the trumpet's mouth."   F Tennyson.

"Alas! what boots——"   Milton's Lycidas. line 64.

THE MERMAIDS

On the shores of Riga,
  Right early in the day,
You may see the little mermaids
  Merrily at play;
Floating on the waters
  In the ebbing tide,
Ocean's loveliest daughters,
  Merrily they ride.

Sometimes you may see them
  In the waning light,
Gently, gently fading
  From our eager sight
With their long fair tresses
  Floating in the breeze;
Their whispers like the sighing
  Of the wind among the trees.

And you may see them sometimes,
  When the moon is on the sea,
In the calm deep midnight,
  Sleeping peacefully:
When all around is dark and still,
  Save the silver-crested sea,
And the moonlight shining in their hair,
  Shining all silently.

But you will never see them
　In the noonday's heat and glare,
When the sun is shining brightly,
　And its glory fills the air.
For then they dive and hide them
　From the heat and blinding light
In the deep, cool waters of the sea,
　Far, far beyond our sight.

But you may hear their voices
　Borne upward from the deep
In low and gentle lullabies,
　Hushing the waves to sleep :
The sailor standeth listening,
　With a tear-drop in his eye,
To their soft and dreamy whispers,
　In the ocean's melody.

Then on some quiet noonday
　Sail slow to Riga's shore,
And hear their gentle voices
　In the ocean's rush and roar ;
And watch them in the evening hour
　Fading from the sight
And gaze upon their dreamless sleep
　In the pale moon's silver light,

THE MERMAIDS

And when in early morning
   You sail from Riga's bay,
You'll see those little mermaids
   Merrily at play.

RIPON—end of 1854.

THE TWO BROTHERS

THERE were two brothers at Twyford school,
  And when they had left the place,
It was, "Will ye learn Greek and Latin?
  Or will ye run me a race?
Or will ye go up to yonder bridge,
  And there we will angle for dace?"

"I'm too stupid for Greek and for
    Latin,
  I'm too lazy by half for a race,
So I'll even go up to yonder bridge,
  And there we will angle for dace."

He has fitted together two joints of his rod,
  And to them he has added another,
And then a great hook he took from his book,
  And ran it right into his brother.

Oh much is the noise that is made among boys
  When playfully pelting a pig,
But a far greater pother was made by his brother,
  When flung from the top of the brigg.

The fish hurried up by the dozens,
   All ready and eager to bite,
For the lad that he flung was so tender and young,
   It quite gave them an appetite.

Said, " Thus shall he wallop about
   And the fish take him quite at their ease,
For me to annoy it was ever his joy,
   Now I'll teach him the meaning of ' Tees ' ! "

The wind to his ear brought a voice,
   " My brother, you didn't had ought ter !
And what have I done that you think it such fun
   To indulge in the pleasure of slaughter ?

" A good nibble or bite is my chiefest delight,
   When I'm merely expected to *see*,
But a bite from a fish is not quite what I wish,
   When I get it performed upon *me*
And just now here's a swarm of dace at my arm,
   And a perch has got hold of my knee !

" For water my thirst was not great at the first,
   And of fish I have had quite sufficien—"

97

"Oh fear not!" he cried, "for whatever betide,
  We are both in the selfsame condition!

"I am sure that our state's very nearly alike,
  (Not considering the question of slaughter)
For I have my perch on the top of the bridge,
  And you have your perch in the water.

"I stick to my perch and your perch
    sticks to you,
  We are really extremely alike;
I've a turn-pike up here, and I very much fear
  You may soon have a turn with a pike."

"Oh grant but one wish! If I'm took by a fish,
  (For your bait is your brother, good man!)
Pull him up if you like, but I hope you will strike
  As gently as ever you can."

"If the fish be a trout, I'm afraid there's no doubt
  I must strike him like lightning that's greased;
If the fish be a pike, I'll engage not to strike,
  'Till I've waited ten minutes at least."

"But in those ten minutes to desolate Fate
    Your brother a victim may fall!"
"I'll reduce it to five, so *perhaps* you'll survive,
    But the chance is exceedingly small."

"Oh hard is your heart for to act such a part,
    Is it iron, or granite, or steel?"
"Why, I really can't say—it is many a day
    Since my heart was accustomed to feel.

"'Twas my heart-cherished wish for to slay many fish,
    Each day did my malice grow worse,
For my heart didn't soften with doing it so often,
    But rather, I should say, the reverse."

"Oh would I were back at Twyford school,
    Learning lessons in fear of the birch!"
"Nay, brother!" he cried, "for whatever betide,
    You are better off here with your perch!

"I am sure you'll allow you are happier now,
    With nothing to do but to play;
And this single line here, it is perfectly clear,
    Is much better than thirty a day!

99

"And as to the rod hanging over your head,
  And apparently ready to fall,
That, you know, was the case, when you lived in that
    place,
  So it need not be reckoned at all.

"Do you see that old trout with a turn-up-nose snout?
  (Just to speak on a pleasanter theme,)
Observe, my dear brother, our love for each other—
  He's the one I like best in the stream.

"To-morrow I mean to invite him to dine,
  (We shall all of us think it a treat,)
If the day should be fine, I'll just *drop him a line*,
  And we'll settle what time we're to meet.

"He hasn't been into society yet,
  And his manners are not of the best,
So I think it quite fair that it should be *my* care
    To see that he's properly dressed."

Many words brought the wind of "cruel" and "kind,"
  And that "man suffers more than the brute":
Each several word with patience he heard,
  And answered with wisdom to boot.

" What ? prettier swimming in the stream,
   Then lying all snugly and flat ?
Do but look at that dish filled with glittering fish,
   Has Nature a picture like that ?

" What ? a higher delight to be drawn from the sight
   Of fish full of life and of glee ?
What a noodle you are ! 'tis delightfuller far
   To kill them than let them go free !

" I know there are people who prate by the hour
   Of the beauty of earth, sky, and ocean ;
Of the birds as they fly, of the fish darting by,
   Rejoicing in Life and in Motion.

" As to any delight to be got from the sight,
   It is all very well for a flat,
But *I* think it all gammon, for hooking a salmon
   Is better than twenty of that !

" They say that a man of a right-thinking mind
   Will *love* the dumb creatures he sees—
What's the use of his mind, if he's never inclined
   To pull a fish out of the Tees ?

"Take my friends and my home—as an outcast I'll
    roam;
Take the money I have in the Bank—
It is just what I wish, but deprive me of *fish*,
    And my life would indeed be a blank!"

Forth from the house his sister came,
    Her brothers for to see,
But when she saw that sight of awe,
    The tear stood in her ee.

"Oh what bait's that upon your hook,
    My brother, tell to me?"
"It is but the fantailed pigeon,
    He would not sing for me."

"Whoe'er would expect a pigeon to sing,
    A simpleton he must be!
But a pigeon-cote is a different thing
    To the coat that there I see!

"Oh what bait's that upon your hook,
    My brother, tell to me?"

"It is but the black-capped bantam,
   He would not dance for me."

"And a pretty dance you are leading him now!"
   In anger answered she,
"But a bantam's cap is a different thing
   To the cap that there I see!

"Oh what bait's that upon your hook
   Dear brother, tell to me?"
"It is my younger brother," he cried,
   "Oh woe and dole is me!

"I's mighty wicked, that I is!
   Or how could such things be?
Farewell, farewell sweet sister,
   I'm going o'er the sea."

"And when will you come back again,
   My brother, tell to me?"
"When chub is good for human food,
   And that will never be!"

She turned herself right round about,
   And her heart brake into three,
Said, "One of the two will be wet through and through,
   And t'other'll be late for his tea!"

CROFT. 1853.

POETRY FOR THE MILLION

THE nineteenth century has produced a new school of music, bearing about the same relation to the genuine article, which the hash or stew of Monday does to the joint of Sunday.

We allude of course to the prevalent practice of diluting the works of earlier composers with washy modern variations, so as to suit the weakened and depraved taste of this generation: this invention is termed " setting " by some, who, scorning the handsome offer of Alexander Smith, to " set this age to music," have determined to set music to this age.

Sadly we admit the stern necessity that exists for such a change : with stern prophetic eye we see looming in the shadowy Future the downfall of the sister Fine Arts. The National Gallery have already subjected some of their finest pictures to this painful operation : Poetry must follow.

That we may not be behind others in forwarding the progress of Civilization, we boldly discard all personal and private feelings, and with quivering pen and tear-dimmed eye, we dedicate the following composition to the Spirit of the Age, and to that noble band of gallant adventurers, who aspire to lead the Van in the great March of Reform.

THE DEAR GAZELLE
ARRANGED WITH VARIATIONS

espressivo
" I NEVER loved a dear gazelle,"
Nor aught beside that cost me much ;
High prices profit those who sell,
But why should *I* be fond of such ?

p.p   *cres :*
" To glad me with his soft black eyes,"
My infant son, from Tooting School,
Thrashed by his bigger playmate, flies ;
And serve him right, the little fool !
con spirito

A Tempo
" But when he came to know me well,"
He kicked me out, her testy sire ;
And when I stained my hair, that Bell
Might note the change, and thus admire

dim :   *cadenza*   D.C.
" And love me, it was sure to die "
A muddy green, or staring blue,
While one might trace, with half an eye,
The still triumphant carrot through.
con dolore

CH: CH: 1855.

105

FROM OUR OWN CORRESPONDENT

"THE first idea that struck us on entrance was, the *extremely select* nature of the assembly.

"One of the earliest arrivals was a gentleman of unquestionable 'ton': the lady who accompanied him excited considerable attention, on entering the room, by her exquisite muslin skirt and slip."

SHE'S ALL MY FANCY PAINTED HIM[1]

A POEM

[This affecting fragment was found in MS., among the papers of the well-known author of " Was it You or I ? " a tragedy, and the two popular novels " Sister and Son," and " The Niece's Legacy, or the Grateful Grandfather."]

SHE'S all my fancy painted him
    (I make no idle boast);
If he or you had lost a limb,
    Which would have suffered most?

He said that you had been to her,
    And seen me here before;
But, in another character,
    She was the same of yore.

There was not one that spoke to us,
    Of all that thronged the street;
So he sadly got into a 'bus,
    And pattered with his feet.

They sent him word I had not gone
    (We know it to be true);
If she should push the matter on,
    What would become of you?

[1 This is a newspaper cutting pasted into the original scrap-book.]

They gave her one, they gave me two,
　　They gave us three or more;
They all returned from him to you,
　　Though they were mine before.

If I or she should chance to be
　　Involved in this affair,
He trusts to you to set them free,
　　Exactly as we were.

It seemed to me that you had been
　　(Before she had this fit)
An obstacle, that came between
　　Him, and ourselves, and it.

Don't let him know she liked them best,
　　For this must ever be
A secret, kept from all the rest,
　　Between yourself and me.

PHOTOGRAPHY EXTRAORDINARY[1]

THE recent extraordinary discovery in Photography, as
applied to the operations of the mind, has reduced the
art of novel-writing to the merest mechanical labour.
We have been kindly permitted by the artist to be present

[1 This is a cutting from a newspaper pasted into the original
scrap-book.]

during one of his experiments; but as the invention has not yet been given to the world, we are only at liberty to relate the results, suppressing all details of chemicals and manipulation.

The operator began by stating that the ideas of the feeblest intellect, when once received on properly prepared paper, could be "developed" up to any required degree of intensity. On hearing our wish that he would begin with an extreme case, he obligingly summoned a young man from an adjoining room, who appeared to be of the very weakest possible physical and mental powers. On being asked what we thought of him, we candidly confessed that he seemed incapable of anything but sleep : our friend cordially assented to this opinion.

The machine being in position, and a mesmeric rapport established between the mind of the patient and the object glass, the young man was asked whether he wished to say anything; he feebly replied "Nothing." He was then asked what he was thinking of, and the answer, as before, was "Nothing." The artist on this pronounced him to be in a most satisfactory state, and at once commenced the operation.

After the paper had been exposed for the requisite time, it was removed and submitted to our inspection ; we found it to be covered with faint and almost illegible characters. A closer scrutiny revealed the following :—

"The eve was soft and dewy mild; a zephyr whispered in the lofty glade, and a few light drops of rain cooled the thirsty soil. At a slow amble, along the primrose-bordered path, rode a gentle-looking and amiable youth, holding a light cane in his delicate hand; the pony moved gracefully beneath him, inhaling as it went the fragrance of the roadside flowers: the calm smile, and languid eyes, so admirably harmonizing with the fair features of the rider, showed the even tenor of his thoughts. With a sweet though feeble voice, he plaintively murmured out the gentle regrets that clouded his breast:—

'Alas! she would not hear my prayer!
Yet it were rash to tear my hair;
Disfigured, I should be less fair.

She was unwise, I may say blind;
Once she was lovingly inclined;
Some circumstance has changed her mind.'

There was a moment's silence; the pony stumbled over a stone in the path, and unseated his rider. A crash was heard among the dried leaves; the youth arose; a slight bruise on his left shoulder, and a disarrangement of his cravat, were the only traces that remained of this trifling accident."

"This," we remarked as we returned the papers, "belongs apparently to the milk-and-water School of

Novels." "You are quite right," our friend replied, "and, in its present state, it is of course utterly unsaleable in the present day: we shall find, however, that the next stage of development will remove it into the strong-minded or Matter-of-Fact School." After dipping it into various acids, he again submitted it to us: it had now become the following :—

"The evening was of the ordinary character, barometer at 'change': a wind was getting up in the wood, and some rain was beginning to fall; a bad look-out for the farmers. A gentleman approached along the bridle-road, carrying a stout knobbed stick in his hand, and mounted on a serviceable nag, possibly worth some £40 or so; there was a settled business-like expression on the rider's face, and he whistled as he rode; he seemed to be hunting for rhymes in his head, and at length repeated, in a satisfied tone, the following composition :—

> 'Well! so my offer was no go!
> She might do worse, I told her so;
> She was a fool to answer 'No.'
>
> However, things are as they stood;
> Nor would I have her if I could,
> For there are plenty more as good.'

At this moment the horse set his foot in a hole, and rolled over; his rider rose with difficulty; he had sustained several severe bruises, and fractured two ribs; it was some time before he forgot that unlucky day."

We returned this with the strongest expression of admiration, and requested that it might now be developed to the highest possible degree. Our friend readily consented, and shortly presented us with the result, which he informed us belonged to the Spasmodic or German School. We perused it with indescribable sensations of surprise and delight.

"The night was wildly tempestuous—a hurricane raved through the murky forest—furious torrents of rain lashed the groaning earth. With a headlong rush—down a precipitous mountain gorge—dashed a mounted horseman armed to the teeth—his horse bounded beneath him at a mad gallop, snorting fire from its distended nostrils as it flew. The rider's knotted brows—rolling eye-balls—and clenched teeth —expressed the intense agony of his mind—weird visions loomed upon his burning brain—while with a mad yell he poured forth the torrent of his boiling passion :—

> 'Firebrands and daggers! hope hath fled!
> To atoms dash the doubly dead!
> My brain is fire—my heart is lead!
>
> Her soul is flint, and what am I?
> Scorch'd by her fierce, relentless eye,
> Nothingness is my destiny!'

There was a moment's pause. Horror! his path ended in a fathomless abyss— * * * A rush—a flash— a crash—all was over. Three drops of blood, two teeth, and a stirrup were all that remained to tell where the wild horseman met his doom."

The young man was now recalled to consciousness, and shown the result of the workings of his mind: he instantly fainted away.

In the present infancy of the art we forbear from further comment on this wonderful discovery; but the mind reels as it contemplates the stupendous addition thus made to the powers of science.

Our friend concluded with various minor experiments, such as working up a passage of Wordsworth into strong, sterling poetry: the same experiment was tried on a passage of Byron, at our request, but the paper came out scorched and blistered all over by the fiery epithets thus produced.

As a concluding remark: *could* this art be applied (we put the question in the strictest confidence)—*could* it, we ask, be applied to the speeches in Parliament? It may be but a delusion of our heated imagination, but we will still cling fondly to the idea, and hope against hope.

HINTS FOR ETIQUETTE; OR, DINING OUT MADE EASY [1]

AS caterers for the public taste, we can conscientiously recommend this book to all diners-out who are perfectly unacquainted with the usages of society. However we may regret that our author has confined himself to warning rather than advice, we are bound in justice to say that nothing here stated will be found to contradict the habits of the best circles. The following examples exhibit a depth of penetration and a fulness of experience rarely met with.

v

In proceeding to the dining-room, the gentleman gives one arm to the lady he escorts—it is unusual to offer both.

*   *   *   *

VIII

The practice of taking soup with the next gentleman but one is now wisely discontinued; but the custom of asking your host his opinion of the weather immediately on the removal of the first course still prevails.

[1 This is a cutting from a newspaper pasted into the original scrap-book.]

IX

To use a fork with your soup, intimating at the same time to your hostess that you are reserving the spoon for the beefsteaks, is a practice wholly exploded.

*   *   *   *

XI

On meat being placed before you, there is no possible objection to your eating it, if so disposed; still in all such delicate cases, be guided entirely by the conduct of those around you.

XII

It is always allowable to ask for artichoke jelly with your boiled venison; however there are houses where this is not supplied.

XIII

The method of helping roast turkey with two carving-forks is practicable, but deficient in grace.

*   *   *   *

XVII

We do not recommend the practice of eating cheese with a knife and fork in one hand and a spoon and wine-glass in the other; there is a kind of awkwardness in the action which no amount of practice can entirely dispel.

*   *   *   *

XXVI

As a general rule, do not kick the shins of the opposite gentleman under the table, if personally unacquainted with him : your pleasantry is liable to be misunderstood —a circumstance at all times unpleasant.

XXVII

Proposing the health of the boy in buttons immediately on the removal of the cloth, is a custom springing from regard to his tender years, rather than from a strict adherence to the rules of etiquette.

NOTICE TO THE PUBLIC

THE two following compositions, " Wilhelm von Schmitz " and " The Lady of the Ladle," were originally published in the " Whitby Gazette," a weekly periodical, price one penny : what opinion the Editor of that paper formed of them may be judged from his farewell address, inserted below.

As the scenery and many of the allusions refer to Whitby, the papers may not prove very intelligible to the general reader ; still, if they succeed in imparting one transient glow of satisfaction to the breast of any individual however humble, or in awakening one sickly smile on the countenance of any reader however disreputable, the author's incessant and exhausting toil of sixteen long years will have been abundantly repaid.

[1] THE PUBLISHER OF THE WHITBY GAZETTE in issuing the last number for the first season, gratefully acknowledges its favourable reception, and although he cannot but own that the literary department as a whole, has not been of a high or specially attractive nature, yet the object originally intended has been realized, namely, the publishing of a List of Lodging Houses and Visitors, for the use of the greatly increased number who have sought health and recreation amid the attractions of this rapidly rising watering-place.

Although as a pecuniary speculation the past would not warrant him in promising its re-appearance, yet, confidently hoping that its usefulness will be more generally owned, he respectfully announces that at the proper season it will again be issued.

Thanks are awarded to those who have taken an interest in its publication and have so kindly furnished materials for its columns, and hopes are entertained that the services of those and other kind friends will again be afforded when the publication is resumed.

[[1] This is a cutting from a newspaper pasted into the original scrap-book.]

WILHELM VON SCHMITZ[1]

CHAPTER III

"Nay, 'tis too much!"

Old Play.

NIGHT, solemn night.

On the present occasion the solemnity of night's approach was rendered far more striking than it is to dwellers in ordinary towns, by that time-honoured custom observed by the people of Whitby, of leaving their streets wholly unlighted: in thus making a stand against the deplorably swift advance of the tide of progress and civilization, they displayed no small share of moral courage and independent judgment. Was it for a people of sense to adopt every new-fangled invention of the age, merely because their neighbours did? It might have been urged, in disparagement of their conduct, that they only injured themselves by it, and the remark would have been undeniably true; but it would only have served to exalt, in the eyes of an admiring nation, their well-earned character of heroic self-denial and uncompromising fixity of purpose.

Headlong and desperate, the love-lorn Poet plunged through the night; now tumbling up against a doorstep, and now half down in a gutter, but ever onward, onward, reckless where he went.

[1 This is a cutting from a newspaper pasted into the original scrap-book.]

In the darkest spot of one of those dark streets, (the nearest lighted shop window being about fifty yards off,) chance threw into his way the very man he fled from, the man whom he hated as a successful rival, and who had driven him to this pitch of frenzy. The waiter, not knowing what was the matter, had followed him to see that he came to no harm, and to bring him back, little dreaming of the shock that awaited him.

The instant the Poet perceived who it was, all his pent-up fury broke forth : to rush upon him, to grasp him by the throat with both hands, to dash him to the ground, and there to reduce him to the extreme verge of suffocation—all this was the work of a moment.

" Traitor ! villain ! malcontent ! regicide ! " he hissed through his closed teeth, taking any abusive epithet that came into his head, without stopping to consider its suitability, " Is it thou ? now shalt thou feel my wrath ! " And doubtless the waiter did experience that singular sensation, whatever it may have been, for he struggled violently with his assailant, and bellowed " murder ! " the instant he recovered his breath.

" Say not so," the Poet sternly answered, as he released him, " it is thou that murderest me." The waiter gathered himself up, and began in great surprise, " Why, Hi never——" " 'Tis a lie ! " the Poet screamed, " she loves thee not ! Me, me alone." " Who ever said she did ? " the other asked, beginning to perceive how matters stood. "Thou! thou saidst it," was the wild reply, "what, villain? acquire her heart? thou never shalt."

The waiter calmly explained himself: "My ope were, sir, to hacquire her Hart of waiting at table, which she do perdigious well, sure-ly: seeing as ow Hi were thinking of happlying for to be ed-waiter at the otel." The Poet's wrath instantly abated, indeed, he looked rather crest-fallen than otherwise; "Excuse my violence," he gently said, "and let us take a friendly glass together." "Hi hagree," was the waiter's generous answer, "but man halive, you've ruinated my coat!"

"Courage!" cried our hero gaily, "thou shalt have a new one anon: aye, and of the best cashmere." "Hm!" said the other, hesitatingly, "well, Hi ardly know——wouldn't hany other stuff——" "I will not buy thee one of any other stuff," returned the Poet, gently but decidedly, and the waiter gave up the point.

Arrived once more at the friendly tavern, the Poet briskly ordered a jorum of punch, and, on its being furnished, called on his friend for a toast. "Hi'll give you," said the waiter, who was of a sentimental turn, however little he looked like it, "hi'll give you— Woman! She doubles our sorrows, and alves our joys." The Poet drained his glass, not caring to correct his companion's mistake, and at intervals during the evening the same inspiring sentiment was repeated. And so the night wore away, and another jorum of punch was ordered, and another.

*   *   *   *   *   *   *

" Hand now hallow me," said the waiter, attempting for about the tenth time that night to rise on to his feet and make a speech, and failing even more signally than he had yet done, " to give a toast for this appy hoccasion. Woman! she doubles——" but at this moment, probably in illustration of his favourite theory, he " doubled " himself up, and so effectually, that he instantly vanished under the table.

Occupying that limited sphere of observation, it is conjectured that he fell to moralizing on human ills in general, and their remedies, for a solemn voice was presently heard to issue from his retreat, proclaiming, feelingly though rather indistinctly, that " when the art of a man is hoppressed with care——" here came a pause, as if he wished to leave the question open to discussion, but as no one present seemed competent to suggest the proper course to be taken in that melancholy contingency, he attempted to supply the deficiency himself with the remarkable statement " she's hall my fancy painted er."

Meanwhile the Poet was sitting, smiling quietly to himself, as he sipped his punch: the only notice he took of his companion's abrupt disappearance was to help himself to a fresh glass, and say, " your health ! " in a cordial tone, nodding to where the waiter ought to have been. He then cried " hear, hear ! " encouragingly, and made an attempt to thump the table with his fist, but missed it. He seemed interested in the question regarding the heart oppressed with care, and winked sagaciously with one eye two or three times, as if there were a good deal he could say on that subject, if he chose: but the second quotation roused him to speech, and he at once broke into the waiter's subterranean soliloquy with an ecstatic fragment from the poem he had been just composing :

" What though the world be cross and crooky ?
Of Life's fair flowers the fairest bouquet
I plucked, when I chose *thee*, my Sukie !

Say, could'st thou grasp at nothing greater
Than to be wedded to a waiter ?
And didst thou deem thy Schmitz a traitor ?

Nay ! the fond waiter was rejected,
And thou, alone, with flower-bedecked head,
Sitting, didst sing of one expected.

And while the waiter, crazed and silly,
Dreamed he had won that priceless lily,
At length he came, thy wished-for Willie.

123

And then thy music took a new key,
For whether Schmitz be boor or duke, he
Is all in all to faithful Sukie!"

He paused for a reply, but a heavy snoring from beneath the table was the only one he got.

B. B.

WILHELM VON SCHMITZ

CHAPTER IV

" Is this the hend ? "
Nicholas Nickleby.

BATHED in the radiance of the newly-risen sun, the billows are surging and bristling below the cliff, along which the Poet is thoughtfully wending his way. It may possibly surprise the reader that he should not ere this have obtained an interview with his beloved Sukie : he may ask the reason ; he will ask in vain : to record with rigid accuracy the progress of events, is the sole duty of the historian : were he to go beyond that, and attempt to dive into the hidden causes of things, the why and the wherefore, he would be trespassing upon the province of the metaphysician.

Scarcely observing, as he passed along, a row of newly built lodging-houses, a spacious Hotel, with excellent stabling and lock-up coach-houses, hot, cold, and shower-baths in the house, an omnibus and cabs attend the arrival and departure of each train,—a mysterious-looking wooden sugar-loaf, perched upon posts, with a handle to it above, suggesting the idea of an umbrella blown inside out,—and a series of grass-plots, shaped like saucers, he reached a small rising ground at the end of the gravel walk, where he found a seat commanding a view of the sea, and here he sunk down wearily.

For a while he gazed dreamily upon the expanse of ocean, then, struck by a sudden thought, he opened a small pocket-book, and proceeded to correct and complete his last poem.   Slowly he muttered to himself the words " death,—saith,—breath,—" impatiently tapping the ground with his foot, " ah, that'll do," he said at last with an air of great relief, " breath " :

> " His barque hath perished in the storm,
>   Whirled by its fiery breath
> On sunken rocks, his stalwart form
>   Was doomed to watery death."

" That last line's good," he continued exultingly, " and on Coleridge's principle of alliteration too, W, D, W, D, ' was doomed to watery death.' "

" Say you so ? " growled a deep voice in his ear, " take care ! what you say will be used in evidence against you,—now it's no use trying that sort of thing, we've got you tight " : this last remark being caused by the struggles of the Poet, naturally indignant at being unexpectedly collared by two men from behind.

" He's confessed to it, constable ? you heard him ? " said one of the two, (who rejoiced in the euphonious title of Muggle, and whom it is almost superfluous to introduce to the reader as the elder traveller of Chapter I,) " it's as much as his life is worth." " I say, stow that—" warmly responded the other, " seems to me the gen'leman was a spouting potry."

"What—what's the matter?" here gasped our unfortunate hero, who had recovered his breath, "you—Muggle—what do you mean by it?"

"Mean by it!" blustered his quondam friend, "what do *you* mean by it, if you come to that? you're an assassin, that's what *you* are! where's the waiter you had with you last night? answer me that!"

"The—the waiter?" slowly repeated the Poet, still stunned by the suddenness of his capture, "why he's dr——"

"I knew it!" cried his friend, who was at him in a moment, and choked up the unfinished word in his throat, "drowned, constable! I told you so—and who did it?" he continued, loosing his grasp a moment to obtain an answer.

The Poet's answer, so far as it could be gathered, (for it came out in a very fragmentary state, and as it were by crumbs, in intervals of choking) was the following: "It was my—my—you'll kill me—fault—I say, fault—I—I gave him—you—you're suffoca—I say,—I gave him——" "—a push, I suppose," concluded the other, who here "shut off" the slender supply of breath he had hitherto allowed his victim, "and he fell in: no doubt. I heard some one had fallen off the bridge last night," turning to the constable, "no doubt this unfortunate waiter. Now mark my words! from this moment I renounce this man as my friend: don't pity him, constable! don't think of letting him go to spare *my* feelings!"

"Don't wex yourself," was the philosophic rejoinder, "I wouldn't let him go—not for to spare the feelings o' twenty sich."

This reply, though it could scarcely be considered complimentary, seemed quite satisfactory to the excited Muggle, who now continued more calmly, "But don't you go talking about poetry, constable, and trying to get him off that way, otherwise you *may* be—mark my words, I say you *may* be, acquitted as adversary before the fact!" a keen love for the use of law-terms, in which however he did not shine, being a marked trait in the character of Muggle.

The constable, who was chewing a straw, made no answer to this extraordinary communication, nor, to say the truth, did he appear at all interested in it. Some convulsive sounds at this moment were heard from the Poet, which, on attentive consideration, were found to be, "The punch—was—was too much—for him—quite—it, quite——"

"Miserable man!" sternly interposed Muggle, "can you jest about it! you gave him a punch, did you? and what then?"

"It quite—quite—upset him," continued the unhappy Schmitz, in a sort of rambling soliloquy, which was here cut short by the impatience of the constable, and the party set forth on their return to the town.

A small knot of people were assembled at the street corner to see the melancholy procession go past: the Poet was on the point of addressing them, and the words "Friends, Romans, countrymen," rose to his lips, but on second thoughts he discarded the phrase, as inapplicable to the present occasion. Before, however, he could pitch upon a sufficient substitute, and while he was yet waving his right arm gracefully up and down in act to speak, a distant cry of " hinnocent ! hinnocent ! " was heard, and an unexpected character burst upon the scene.

The first impression the Poet formed of him was, that some baker's apprentice had gone mad, had been stopped in an attempt to drown himself, and escaped from his friends : the being in question had a white apron twisted about him in a mysterious manner, his hair was dripping with water, his eyes wild and rolling, and his manner desperate : and his whole vocabulary seemed to consist of the single word " hinnocent ! " which he repeated without any pause, and with surprising emphasis.

A path was made for him to pass through the mob, and on arriving opposite the constable he suddenly broke into a speech, far more remarkable for energetic delivery, than for grammatical accuracy : " Hi've only just erd of it—Hi were asleep under table—avin taking more punch nor Hi could stand—him's as hinnocent as Hi ham—howing to the punch, which uncommon good it were, but that's neither ere nor there—dead hindeed! Hi'd like to see im as said it!—Hi'm haliver than yer, a precious sight!"

This speech produced different effects upon its hearers: the constable calmly released his man, and with the parting words, "All right, young 'un; wish you joy," turned on his heel whistling, and departed: the bewildered Muggle plunged his hands into his pockets, and muttered "Impossible! conspiracy—perjury—have it tried at assizes": while the happy Poet rushed into the arms of his deliverer, crying in a broken voice, "No, never from this hour to part, We'll live and love so true!" a sentiment which the waiter did not echo with the cordiality that might have been expected.

From this transport of gratitude and delight he awoke to feel a gentle touch on his shoulder, and to see the fair Sukie herself bending over him: their meeting was—, but on second thoughts we abandon the description as hopeless: it transcends the feeble powers of language.

It was in the course of the same day, when Wilhelm and his Sukie were sitting conversing with the waiter and a few mutual friends, that the penitent Muggle suddenly entered the room, placed a folded paper on the knees of Schmitz, pronounced in a hollow tone the affecting words " be happy ! ", vanished, and was no more seen.

After perusing the paper, the Poet suddenly rose to his feet, and the grace of his attitude struck all present: (one of his friends afterwards compared it to the Belvidere Apollo, but the simile is supposed to be exaggerated). The inspiration of the moment roused him into unconscious and extempore verse, positively for the first and last time within the memory of man.

> " My Sukie! he hath bought, yea, Muggle's self,
> Convinced at last of deeds unjust and foul,
> The licence of a vacant public-house,
> Which, with it's chattels, site, and tenement,
> He hands us over,—we are licensed here,
> Even in this document, to sell to all
> Snuff, pepper, vinegar, to sell to all
> Ale, porter, spirits, but—observe you well—
> ' *Not* to be drunk upon the premises! '
> Oh, Sukie! heed it well! in other places,
> Even as thou listest, be intoxicate :
> Drink without limit whiles thou art abroad,
> But never, never, in thy husband's house! "

So we leave him : his after happiness who dares to doubt ? has he not Sukie ? and having her, he is content, or, to use the more graceful and expressive language of the sympathetic waiter, with whose words we conclude the tale, he " henvies no hother man on herth, owever many may ate *im*."

B. B.

THE END

WHITBY. 1854.

THE LADY OF THE LADLE

The youth at eve had drunk his fill
Where stands the " Royal " on the Hill,
And long his midday stroll had made
On the so-called " Marine Parade "—
(Meant, I presume, for seamen brave,
Whose " march is on the mountain wave "—
'Twere just the bathing-place for him
Who stays on land till he can swim—)
Yes, he had strayed into the town,
And paced each alley up and down,
Where still, so narrow grew the way,
The very houses seemed to say,
Nodding to friends across the street,
" One struggle more and we shall meet."

And he had scaled that awful stair
That soars from earth to upper air,
Where rich and poor alike must climb,
And walk the treadmill for a time—
That morning he had dressed with care,
And put pomatum in his hair;
He was, the loungers all agreed,
A very heavy swell indeed:
Men thought him, as he swaggered by,
Some scion of nobility,

And never dreamed, so cold his look,
That he had loved—and loved a Cook.
Upon the beach he stood and sighed,
All heedless of the rising tide;
Thus sang he to the listening main,
And soothed his sorrows with the strain:

Coronach

" She is gone by the *Hilda*,
  She is lost unto Whitby,
And her name is Matilda,
  Which my heart it was smit by.
Tho' I take the *Goliah*,
  Yet I learn to my sorrow,
That ' it won't,' says the crier,
  ' Be off till to-morrow.'

" She had called me her ' Neddy,'
  (Though there mayn't be much in it),
And I should have been ready
  If she'd waited a minute.
I was following behind her,
  When, if you recollect, I
Merely ran back to find a
  Gold pin for my neck-tie.

134

"Rich dresser of suet!
   Prime hand at a sassage!
I have lost thee, I rue it,
   And my fare for the passage!
Perhaps *she* thinks it funny,
   Aboard of the *Hilda*,
But I've lost purse and money,
   And thee, oh my 'Tilda!"

His pin of gold the youth undid,
And in his waistcoat-pocket hid,
Then gently folded hand in hand,
And dropped asleep upon the sand.

                B. B. WHITBY. *Aug:* 1854.

STUDIES FROM ENGLISH POETS Nº III

"He gave it to his father."   Ossian.

LAYS OF MYSTERY, IMAGINATION, AND HUMOUR

N O. I.

THE PALACE OF HUMBUG

for the end of 1855.

I DREAMT I dwelt in marble halls,
And each damp thing that creeps and crawls
Went wobble-wobble on the walls.

Faint odours of departed cheese,
Blown on the dank, unwholesome breeze,
Awoke the never-ending sneeze.

Strange pictures decked the arras drear,
Strange characters of woe and fear,
The humbugs of the social sphere.

One showed a vain and noisy prig,
That shouted empty words and big
At him that nodded in a wig.

And one, a dotard grim and grey,
Who wasteth childhood's happy day
In work more profitless than play.

136

Whose icy breast no pity warms,
Whose little victims sit in swarms,
And slowly sob on lower forms.

And one, a green thyme-honoured Bank,
Where flowers are growing wild and rank,
Like weeds that fringe a poisoned tank.

All birds of evil omen there
Flood with rich Notes the tainted air,
The witless wanderer to snare.

The fatal Notes neglected fall,
No creature heeds the treacherous call,
For all those goodly Strawn Baits Pall.

The wandering phantom broke and fled,
Straightway I saw within my head
A Vision of a ghostly bed,

Where lay two worn decrepit men,
The fictions of a lawyer's pen,
Who never more might breathe again.

The servingman of Richard Roe
Wept, inarticulate with woe :
She wept, that waited on John Doe.

"Oh rouse," I urged, "the waning sense
With tales of tangled evidence,
Of suit, demurrer, and defence."

"Vain," she replied, "such mockeries :
For morbid fancies, such as these,
No suits can suit, no plea can please."

And bending o'er that man of straw,
She cried in grief and sudden awe,
Not inappropriately, "Law !"

The well-remembered voice he knew,
He smiled, he faintly muttered "Sue !"
(Her very name was legal too.)

The night was fled, the dawn was nigh :
A hurricane went raving by,
And swept the Vision from mine eye.

138

Vanished that dim and ghostly bed,
(The hangings, tape; the tape was red:)
'Tis o'er, and Doe and Roe are dead!

Oh yet my spirit inly crawls,
What time it shudderingly recalls
That horrid dream of marble halls!

OXFORD. 1855.

STANZA OF ANGLO-SAXON POETRY

THIS curious fragment reads thus in modern characters:

TWAS BRYLLYG, AND THE SLYTHY TOVES
DID GYRE AND GYMBLE IN THE WABE:
ALL MIMSY WERE THE BOROGOVES;
AND THE MOME RATHS OUTGRABE.

The meanings of the words are as follows:
BRYLLYG (derived from the verb to BRYL or BROIL).
"the time of broiling dinner, i.e. the close of the afternoon."

139

SLYTHY (compounded of SLIMY and LITHE). "Smooth and active."

TOVE. A species of Badger. They had smooth white hair, long hind legs, and short horns like a stag : lived chiefly on cheese.

GYRE, verb (derived from GYAOUR or GIAOUR, "a dog "). "To scratch like a dog."

GYMBLE (whence GIMBLET). "To screw out holes in anything."

WABE (derived from the verb to SWAB or SOAK). "The side of a hill " (from its being *soaked* by the rain).

MIMSY (whence MIMSERABLE and MISERABLE). "Un-happy."

BOROGOVE. An extinct kind of Parrot. They had no wings, beaks turned up, and made their nests under sun-dials : lived on veal.

MOME (hence SOLEMOME, SOLEMONE, and SOLEMN). "Grave."

RATH. A species of land turtle. Head erect : mouth like a shark : the fore legs curved out so that the animal walked on its knees : smooth green body : lived on swallows and oysters.

OUTGRABE, past tense of the verb to OUTGRIBE. (It is connected with the old verb to GRIKE or SHRIKE, from which are derived " shriek " and " creak.") "Squeaked."

Hence the literal English of the passage is : " It was evening, and the smooth active badgers were scratching and boring holes in the hill-side : all unhappy were the parrots ; and the grave turtles squeaked out."

There were probably sun-dials on the top of the hill, and the " borogoves " were afraid that their nests would be undermined.   The hill was probably full of the nests of " raths," which ran out, squeaking with fear, on hearing the " toves " scratching outside.   This is an obscure, but yet deeply-affecting, relic of ancient Poetry.—ED.

CROFT.   1855.

LAYS OF MYSTERY, IMAGINATION, AND HUMOUR

NO. 2.

THE THREE VOICES

The First Voice

WITH hands tight clenched through matted hair,
He crouched in trance of dumb despair,
There came a breeze from out the air.

It passed athwart the glooming flat,
It fanned his forehead as he sat,
It lightly bore away his hat:

All to the feet of one who stood
Like maid enchanted in a wood,
Frowning as darkly as she could.

With huge umbrella, lank and brown,
Unerringly she pinned it down,
Right through the centre of the crown.

Then, with an aspect cold and grim,
Regardless of its battered brim,
She took it up and gave it him.

Awhile like one in dreams he stood,
Then faltered forth his gratitude
In words just short of being rude.

For it had lost its shape and shine,
And it had cost him four and nine,
And he was going out to dine.

With grave indifference to his speech,
Fixing her eyes upon the beach,
She said, " Each gives to more than each."

He raised his eyes in sudden awe,
And stammered out " Thy wish is Law,"
Yet knew not what he said it for.

" If that be so," she straight replied,
" Each heart with each doth coincide :
What boots it? for the world is wide."

And he, not wishing to appear
Less wise, said " This material Sphere
Is but Attributive Idea."

But when she asked him, " Wherefore so ? "
He felt his very whiskers glow,
And frankly owned, " I do not know."

While, like broad waves of golden grain,
Or sunlit hues on cloistered pane,
His colour came and went again.

Pitying his obvious distress,
Yet with a tinge of bitterness,
She said, " The More exceeds the Less."

" A truth of such undoubted weight,"
He urged, " and so extreme in date
It were superfluous to state."

Roused into sudden passion, she,
In tone of stern malignity,
" To others, yes : but not to thee."

Then proudly folded arm in arm,
But when he urged, " I meant no harm,"
Once more her speech grew mild and calm.

" Thought in the mind doth still abide :
That is by Intellect supplied,
And within that Idea doth hide.

" He who doth yearn the Truth to know
Still further inwardly may go,
And find Idea from Notion flow.

" And thus the chain that sages sought
Is to a glorious circle wrought,
For Notion hath its source in Thought."

When he, with racked and whirling brain,
Feebly implored her to explain,
She simply said it all again.

Wrenched with an agony intense,
He spake, neglecting Sound and Sense,
And careless of all consequence :

" Mind—I believe—is Essence—Ent—
Abstract—that is—an Accident—
Which we—that is to say—I meant——"

146

Thus far he panted, wild and flushed,
But when his speech was somewhat hushed,
She looked at him, and he was crushed.

It needed not her calm reply,
She did the business with her eye,
And he could neither fight nor fly,

While she dissected, word by word,
His speech, half guessed at and half heard,
As might a cat a little bird :

Then, having wholly overthrown
His views, and stripped them to the bone,
Proceeded to unfold her own.

So passed they on with even pace,
Yet gradually one might trace
A Shadow growing on his face.

The Second Voice

THEY walked beside the wave-worn beach,
Her tongue was very apt to teach,
And now and then he did beseech

She would abate her dulcet tone,
Because the talk was all her own,
And he was dull as any drone.

She urged, " No knife is like a fork,"
And ceaseless flowed her dreary talk,
Tuned to the footfall of a walk.

Her voice was very full and rich,
And when at last she asked him " Which ? "
It mounted to its highest pitch.

He a bewildered answer gave,
Drowned in the sullen moaning wave,
Lost in the echoes of the cave.

He answered her he knew not what;
Like shaft from bow at random shot
He spoke, but she regarded not.

She waited not for his reply,
But with a downward leaden eye
Went on as if he were not by.

Sound argument and grave defence,
Strange questions raised on " Why ? " and " Whence ? "
And weighted down with common sense.

" Shall Man be Man ? and shall he miss
Of other thoughts no thought but this,
Harmonious dews of sober bliss ?

" What boots it ? Shall his fevered eye
Through towering nothingness descry
This grisly phantom hurry by ?

" And hear dumb shrieks that fill the air,
See mouths that gape, and eyes that stare
And redden in the dusky glare ?

" The meadows breathing amber light,
The darkness toppling from the height,
The feathery train of granite Night?

" Shall he, grown grey among his peers,
Through the thick curtain of his tears
Catch glimpses of his earlier years?

" And hear the sounds he knew of yore,
Old shufflings on the sanded floor,
Old footsteps kicking at the door?

" Yet still before him as he flies
One pallid form shall ever rise,
And, bodying forth in glassy eyes

" A dim reflex of vanished good,
Low peering through the tangled wood,
Shall freeze the current of his blood."

Still from each fact, with skill uncouth
And savage rapture, like a tooth
She wrenched some slow, reluctant truth.

Till, like some silent water-mill
When summer suns have dried the rill,
She reached a full-stop, and was still.

Dead calm succeeded to the fuss,
As when the overladen bus
Has reached the railway terminus;

When, for the tumult of the street
Is heard the engine's stifled beat,
The wary tread of porters' feet.

With glance that ever sought the ground,
She moved her lips without a sound,
And every now and then she frowned.

He gazed upon the sleeping sea,
And joyed in its tranquillity,
And in that silence dead, but she

To muse a little space did seem,
Then, like the echo of a dream,
Harped back upon her threadbare theme.

Still an attentive ear he lent,
But could not fathom what she meant,
She was not deep, nor eloquent.

He marked the ripple on the sand;
The even swaying of her hand
Was all that he could understand.

He left her, and he turned aside;
He sat and watched the coming tide
Across the shores so newly dried.

He wondered at the waters clear,
The breeze that whispered in his ear,
The billows heaving far and near,

And why he had so long preferred
To hang upon her every word,
" In truth," he said, " it was absurd."

[*The Third Voice.*]

Not long this transport held its place:
Within a little moment's space
Quick tears were raining down his face.

His heart stood still, aghast with fear,
A wordless voice, nor far nor near,
He seemed to hear and not to hear.

" Tears kindle not the doubtful spark:
If so, why not? Of this remark
The bearings are profoundly dark."

" Her speech," he said, " hath caused this pain:
Easier I count it to explain
The jargon of the howling main;

" Or, stretched beside some sedgy brook,
To con, with inexpressive look,
An unintelligible book."

154

Low spake the voice within his head
In words imagined more than said,
Soundless as ghost's intended tread.

"If thou art duller than before,
Why quittedst thou the voice of lore?
Why not endure, expecting more?"

"Rather than that," he groaned aghast,
"I'd writhe in depths of cavern vast,
Some loathly vampire's rich repast."

"'Twere hard," it answered, "themes immense
To coop within the narrow fence
That rings thy scant intelligence."

"Not so," he urged, "nor once alone:
But there was that within her tone
Which chilled me to the very bone.

"Her style was anything but clear
And most unpleasantly severe;
Her epithets were very queer.

" And yet, so grand were her replies,
I could not choose but deem her wise,
I did not dare to criticize.

" Nor did I leave her till she went
So deep in tangled argument
That all my powers of thought were spent."

A little whisper inly slid,
" Yet truth is truth : you know you did : "
A little wink beneath the lid.

And, sickened with excess of dread,
Prone to the dust he bent his head,
And lay like one three-quarters dead.

Forth went the whisper like a breeze ;
Left him amid the wondering trees,
Left him by no means at his ease.

Once more he weltered in despair,
With hands through denser-matted hair
More tightly clenched than then they were.

When, bathed in dawn of living red,
Majestic frowned the mountain head,
" Tell me my fault," was all he said.

When, at high noon, the blazing sky
Scorched in his head each haggard eye,
Then keenest rose his weary cry.

And when at eve th' unpitying Sun
Smiled grimly on the solemn fun,
" Alack ! " he sighed, " what *have* I done ? "

But saddest, darkest was the sight,
When the cold grasp of leaden Night
Dashed him to earth and held him tight.

Tortured, unaided, and alone,
Thunders were silence to his groan,
Bagpipes sweet music to its tone :

" What ? ever thus, in dismal round,
Shall Pain and Mystery profound
Pursue me like a sleepless hound

" With crimson-dashed and eager jaws?
Me, still in ignorance of the cause,
Unknowing what I brake of laws? "

The whisper to his ear did seem
Like echoed flow of silent stream,
Or shadow of forgotten dream,

The whisper, trembling in the wind:
" Her fate with thine was intertwined,"
So spake it in his inner mind:

" Each orbed on each a baleful star,
Each proved the other's blight and bar,
Each unto each were best, most far;

" Yea, each to each was worse than foe,
Thou, a scared dullard, gibbering low,
And she, an avalanche of woe."

LAYS OF MYSTERY, IMAGINATION, AND HUMOUR

NO. 3.

TOMMY'S DEAD

[Written Dec. 31, 1847. There is a poem by Sydney Dobell with the same name, and something like this — but not very.]

Iт's the last night of the year, boys,

You may bring out the bread and beer, boys,

We've nought else to do to-night, boys,

This crust is too hard to bite, boys,

Is the donkey all right in the stable, boys?

Set two or three chairs round the table, boys,

We must have some'at to eat afore we go, boys,

Stick another coal on the fire or so, boys,

For the night's very cold,

And I'm very old,

And Tommy's dead.

Will somebody go and call t'owd wife, boys?

And just, while you're about it, fetch another knife, boys,

Get the loaf and cut me a slice, boys,

And how about the cheese, is it nice, boys?

I asked just now for a slice of bread, boys,

I say—*did you hear what I said, boys?*

There's no end of crumbs, sweep up the floor, boys,
Mind you don't forget to bar the door, boys,
For the night's very cold, boys,
And I'm very old, boys,
And Tommy's dead.

Is there any more beer in the jug, boys?
You may as well fill up my mug, boys,
Is there any left still? no, I drank it, boys,
I shall want an extra blanket, boys,
I'm an early body, you mun wake me in t'morning, boys,
Not that I can get up without warning, boys,
I'm not the sort that wakes all of a minute, boys,
When I'm once in my bed I likes to stop in it, boys,
For the night's very cold,
And I'm very old,
And Tommy's dead.

Come, cheer up your old daddy like men, boys,
Why, I declare it's nigh upon half-past ten, boys!
Bread's not much, I'd rather have had some tripe, boys,
D'ye think there's time for a quiet pipe, boys?
There'd be beer enough, if it hadn't been spilt, boys,
I wish I were snug under my quilt, boys,
I does so like having a talk o' nights, boys!
Ah! boys, you're young, *I've* seen a pack o' sights, boys,

When you've lived as long as I, you'll know what it is,
    boys,
Lads like you think it's all to be done in a whiz, boys,
Well, you may carry me upstairs, it's so late, boys,
If it wasn't for the beer, I'm not much weight, boys,
My gout's not so well, so mind how you go, boys,
Some of you'll catch it, if you tread upon my toe, boys,
Gently now, don't trip up on the mat, boys,
There, I told you so, you stupids you, take *that*, boys !
It's good for you, and keeps my hands warm, boys,
I shan't apologize—quite an unnecessary form, boys,
For the night's very cold,
And I'm very old,
And Tommy's dead.

[*Additional Note.*—The last three lines of each paragraph, and the second line of the poem, (perhaps the first as well,) are by Sydney Dobell. For the rest the Editor is responsible: he has taken a less melancholy view of the subject than the original writer did, in support of which theory he begs to record his firm conviction that " Tommy " was a cat. Recollections of its death cause a periodical gloom to come over the father's mind, accompanied always by the other two grounds of complaint which appear to have continually weighed upon him, cold and age: this gloom, we find, was only to be dispelled by one of three things, supper, the prospect of bed, and ill-temper.

There is something very instructive in the fact that the boys are never rude enough to interrupt, and probably never attend till he suggests going to bed, when they carry out his wishes with affectionate, almost unseemly, haste.]

ODE TO DAMON

(FROM CHLOË, WHO UNDERSTOOD HIS MEANING)

Oh do not forget the day when we met
  At the Lowther Arcade in the City,
When you *said* I was plain and excessively vain,
  But I knew that you *meant* I was pretty.

Oh forget not the hour when I purchased the flour,
  (For the dumplings, you know,) and the suet,
While the apples I told my dear Damon to hold,
  (Just to see if you knew how to do it.)

Likewise call to your mind how you left *me* behind
  And went off in a bus with the pippins,
When you *said* you'd forgot, but I knew you had *not*,
  (It was merely to save the odd threepence.)

Then recall your delight in the dumplings that night,
  (Though you *said* they were tasteless and doughy,)
But you winked as you spoke, and I saw that the joke,
  (*If it was one*,) was meant for your Chloë.

And remember the moment when my cousin Joe meant
  To show us the Great Exhibition,
You proposed a short cut, and we found the thing shut,
  (We were two hours too late for admission.)

Your " short cut," dear, we found took us *seven miles
  round*,
  (And Joe said *exactly* what we did,)
Well, *I* helped you out then : (it was *just* like you men,
  Not an atom of sense when it's needed !)

You said " what's to be done ? " and *I* thought you in fun,
  (Never dreaming you were such a ninny,)
" Home directly ! " said I, and *you* paid for the fly,
  (And I *think* that you gave him a guinea.)

Well ! *that* notion, you said, had not entered your head,
  You proposed, " The best thing, as we've come, is
(Since it opens again in the morning at ten,)
  " To wait," *oh you prince of all dummies !*

And when Joe asked you " Why, if a man were to die
  Just as *you* ran a sword through his middle,
You'd be hung for the crime ? " and you said, " give me
  time,"
  And brought to your Chloë the riddle,

Why, remember, you dunce, how I solved it at once,
  (The question that Joe had referred to you,)
Why, I told you the cause was " the force of the laws,"
  And you said " *it had never occurred to you !* "

This instance will show that your brain is too slow,
  And, (though your exterior is showy,)
Yet so arrant a goose can be no sort of use
  To Society—*come to your Chloë !*

You'll find *no one* like me who can manage to see
  Your meaning, you talk so obscurely :
Why, if once *I* were gone, how *would* you get on ?
  Come, you know what *I* mean, Damon, surely !

A monument—men all agree—
Am I in all sincerity,
  Half cat, half hindrance made.
If head and tail removed should be,
Then most of all you strengthen me ;
Replace my head, the stand you see
  On which my tail is laid.

LAYS OF MYSTERY, IMAGINATION, AND HUMOUR

NO. 4.

MELANCHOLETTA

WITH saddest music all day long
 She soothed her secret sorrow;
At night she sighed "I fear 'twas wrong
 Such cheerful words to borrow.
Dearest! a sweeter, sadder song
 I'll sing to thee to-morrow."

I thanked her, but I could not say
 That I was glad to hear it;
I left the house at break of day
 And did not venture near it
Till time, I hoped, had worn away
 Her grief, for nought could cheer it.

My dismal sister! couldst thou know
 The wretched home thou keepest!
Thy brother, drowned in daily woe,
 Is thankful when thou sleepest,
For if I laugh, however low,
 When thou'rt awake, thou weepest.

Melancholetta ! what a word !
   Far better Julius Cæsar,
But, though in youth, I've always heard,
   They christened her Theresa,
" Melancholetta " she preferred,
   And I was glad to please her.

I took my sister t'other day—
   Excuse the slang expression—
To Sadlers Wells to see the play,
   In hopes the new impression
Might in her thoughts, from grave to gay
   Effect some slight digression.

I asked three friends of mine from town
   To join us in our folly,—
In hopes their liveliness might drown
   My sister's melancholy—
The lively Jones, the sportive Brown,
   And Robinson the jolly.

The maid announced the meal in tones
  Of mirth, which I had taught her;
They acted on my sister's moans
  Much like a fire on water—
I rushed to Jones, the lively Jones,
  And begged him to escort her.

" If I'm the man so honourëd——"
  He said in accents cheerful,
" Allow me, miss——" She raised her head,
  With countenance all tearful—
" If I be he——" " Boo! hoo!" she said;
  Matters were getting fearful.

I urged " you're wasting time, you know,
  Delay will spoil the venison."
" My heart is wasted with my woe,
  There is —— I stood in Venice, on
The Bridge of Sighs," she quoted low
  From Byron and from Tennyson.

I won't detail the soup and fish
   In solemn silence swallowed,
The sobs that ushered in each dish
   And its departure followed,
Nor yet my suicidal wish
   To *be* the cheese I hollowed.

Some desperate attempts were made
   To start a conversation—
" Pray, miss," the lively Jones essayed,
   " Which kind of recreation,
Hunting, or fishing, have you made
   Your special occupation ? "

Her lips curved downwards instantly,
   As if of Indian-rubber,
" Hounds *in full cry* I like," said she,
   (Oh ! how I longed to snub her !)
" For fish, a whale's the sport for me,
   It is so full of blubber ! "

The first performance was King John;
   "It's dull," she wept, "and so-so!"
Awhile I let her moans go on;
   She said "they soothed her woe so!"
At length the curtain rose upon
   Bombastes Furioso.

In vain I nudged, in vain I tried
   To rouse her into laughter;
Her tearful glances wandered wide
   From orchestra to rafter—
"*Tier upon tier!*" she said, and sighed,
   And silence followed after.

That very night I laid a plan
   In utter desperation,
And felt myself another man
   In fond anticipation,
And long before the day began
   Had reached the railway-station.

Since then, though I can scarce afford,
  (I took so little money),
To pay for lodging or for board,
  For butter or for honey,
My spirits are so much restored,
  I'm sometimes almost funny.

I live by hook, or else by crook;
  I lodge at present up a
Three-story-back; my favourite book
  Is Martin Farquhar Tupper;
My landlady, a famous cook,
  Fries bacon for my supper.

But if my supper is not light—
  A pardonable error,
(My doctor says, and he is right;
  His name, believe me, 's Ferrer—)
Why then *she* comes in dreams at night
  And fills my soul with terror.

The other night I tried a slice
   Of melon, and I eat a
Large quantity, it proved so nice—
   That night in dreams I met her,
Green as a melon, cold as ice,
   " Dearest ! " she moaned, " art better ?
Thy melon I—will that suffice ?
   Or must I add—choletta ? "

STUDIES FROM ENGLISH POETS Nº IV

" She did so; but 'tis doubtful how or whence — " *Keats.*

172

THE WILLOW TREE

(WRITTEN TO AN OLD ENGLISH AIR)

THE morn was bright, the steeds were light,
  The wedding guests were gay :
Young Ellen stood within the wood,
  And watched them troop away.
She scarcely saw the gallant train,
  The teardrop dimmed her ee ;
Unheard the maiden did complain
  Beneath the willow tree.

" Oh Robin, thou didst love me well,
  But on a fatal day
She came, the lady Isabel,
  And stole thy heart away.
My tears are vain : I live again
  In days that used to be,
When I could meet thy welcome feet
  Beneath the willow tree.

" Oh willow grey, I may not stay
  Till Spring renew thy leaf ;
But I will hide myself away
  And nurse a hopeless grief.

It shall not dim Life's joys for him,
   My tears he shall not see:
While he is by, I'll come not nigh
   My weeping willow tree.

"But when I die, oh let me lie
   Within thy precious shade,
That he may loiter careless by,
   Where I am lowly laid:
And let the white white marble tell,
   If he should stoop to see,
'Here lies a maid who loved thee well,
   Beneath the willow tree.'"

FACES IN THE FIRE

(In *All the Year Round*, No. 42.)

I WATCH the drowsy night expire,
And Fancy paints at my desire
Her magic pictures in the fire.

An island farm, 'mid seas of corn
Swayed by the wandering breath of morn—
The happy spot where I was born.

The picture fadeth in its place,
And fitfully I seem to trace
The shifting semblance of a face.

'Tis now a little childish form,
Red lips for kisses pouted warm,
And elf-locks tangled in the storm—

'Tis now a grave and gentle maid,
At her own beauty half afraid,
Shrinking, and willing to be stayed—

175

'Tis now a matron with her boys,
Dear centre of domestic joys;
I seem to hear the merry noise.

Oh, time was young, and life was warm,
When first I saw that fairy form,
Her dark hair fluttering in the storm;

And fast and free these pulses played
When last I met that gentle maid,
When last her hand in mine was laid.

Those locks of jet are turned to grey,
And she is strange and far away
That might have been mine own today.

That might have been my own, my dear,
Through many and many a happy year,
That might have sat beside me here.

Aye, changeless through the changing scene,
The ghostly whisper rings between,
The dark refrain of " might have been."

FACES IN THE FIRE

The race is o'er I might have run,
The deeds are past I might have done,
And sere the wreath I might have won.

Sunk is the last faint, flickering blaze :
The vision of departed days
Is vanished even as I gaze ;

The pictures with their ruddy light
Are changed to dust and ashes white,
And I am left alone with night.

January. 1860.

REVIEW [1]

From *The Illustrated Times*, Jan. 28/60.

N.B.—The concluding sentence is *not* by the Editor of this Magazine.

PHOTOGRAPHIC EXHIBITION

THERE is very little novelty to call for notice this year, either in subject, or mode of treatment, or chemical process. In the last respect—with some few exceptions, as Jaupenot's and Fothergill's process, collodio-albumen, &c.—the old collodion process constitutes the staple of the exhibition.

The merits and demerits of photographs are, generally speaking, so entirely chemical as to leave little subject for art-criticism. In the quality of chemicals employed the photographer has generally no further concern than in the choice of a chemist; and in such subjects as copies of painting, &c., there is really nothing by which the skill, or want of skill, of the artist himself can be tested. All is done for him. The chief merit of which photographs are capable as chemical productions is sensitiveness of collodion, or other vehicle, and capability of reproducing minute details. This is best tested by foliage and old stonework—foliage especially, as the green presents an obstacle to the

[¹ This is a cutting from the paper mentioned below, pasted into the original scrap-book.]

photographer which has never been perfectly overcome. The best examples of successful treatment of this may be found in Messrs. Cundall and Downes' No. 31, Mr. L. Smith's 23 and 47, Lieut. Holder's No. 66 (though suffering a little from a want of light), and Mr. Robinson's Nos. 73 and 61 ; the latter is, perhaps, the best specimen of this year. In stonework we would call especial notice to Messrs. Bisson's beautiful pictures —(Nos. 30, 34, 35, 36)—nothing can exceed the perfection of detail exhibited by the roof in No. 30 ; and 35 contains a most successful moonlight effect, though no doubt taken in sunlight. Then there are those of Messrs. Cundall and Downes (No. 40) ; Mr. Barnes (No. 17), where the crumbling stonework of the old college fronts is most truthfully rendered ; Mr. Grice (21), all Mr. Piper's ; while, perhaps, the best specimen of detail in architecture and foliage combined is to be found in Mr. Bedford No. 432. As similar subjects we may call attention to Mr. White's 155 and Mr. Fenton's 121 and 145 ; in the latter he has most successfully contended with the additional difficulty of winter light. However, this merit of sensitiveness of collodion may be carried to an extreme, so as to fail in giving the necessary contrast of light and shade, and so to produce a general flat effect. An instance of this may be seen in Mr. Fenton's 130.

The artist himself is mainly responsible in views for

choice of point of view and time of day, and (occasionally) the arrangement of foreground accessories; in such subjects as copies of pictures, &c., for focussing alone; and in portraits, for choice of light, altitude, and grouping.

As instances of taste in choice of view Lord Alfred Churchill's 234 and Mr. Bedford's 238 are well worthy of notice; the former is a thoroughly poetical picture. In the upper picture of 238 the tree in the foreground is perfectly placed, and in the lower remarkable taste has been shown in getting the mass of white formed by the cottage and the cascade just far enough out of the centre to avoid stiffness of composition, and yet not so far as to overbalance the picture by an excess of light on one side; two other good specimens of this may be found in Messrs. Cundall and Downes' 281, and Mr. Mudd's 315.

Instances of good choice of light may be found in Messrs. Maull and Polyblank (No. 5), Mr. Grice (21), Mr. Nudd (37), and Mr. Fenton (150); the last, an interior, is an especially difficult subject.

For good focussing Mr. White's No. 155 may be taken as an instance. This picture is excellent in every way, the collodion having been perfectly sensitive, and a very still day chosen for taking the picture, thus avoiding the too common fault of woolly foliage. The facsimiles of music by Mr. Rippingham (Nos. 558, 561, and 562), and the copy of a map which faces the spectator on entering, are also first-rate.

In taking portraits a well-arranged light is of paramount importance. We have already noticed a remarkable instance of this in No. 5, and another may be found in Mr. Hering's 237, and Messrs. Watkins' 2 and 26. This point is of especial importance, as without it all softness of feature is hopeless.

The grouping of Messrs. Hennah and Kent's 312, and Mr. Robinson's 98 and 493, is especially good. In all the important result of unity of picture has been obtained by giving to the different figures one object of attention ; thus, the cricketing group in 312 may be supposed to be watching a match going on behind the spectator, and in 98 some object to the right has evidently diverted for a moment the attention which would naturally be directed to the spectator himself.

In single portraits the chief difficulty to be overcome is the natural placing of the hands ; within the narrow limits allowed by the focussing power of the lens there are not many attitudes into which they naturally fall, while, if the artist attempts the arrangement himself, he generally produces the effect of the proverbial bashful young man in society who finds for the first time that his hands are an incumbrance, and cannot remember what he is in the habit of doing with them in private life. Mr. Hering's portraits generally are specimens of what may be done in overcoming this difficulty. His portraits of children in No. 327 are nearly all excellent, while the two end ones, and the third from the left in the upper row, are as nearly perfection in this line of art as the present state of photography admits of; the last-mentioned picture (with the trifling drawback of an awkward pose of the right hand) is not surpassed by any in the room. Among pictures of this sort Messrs. Lock and Whitfield also deserve notice, especially the child in profile No. 231, and the same exquisitely coloured in 331. The colouring itself does not of course constitute a branch of photography. Beautiful instances of this may be found in Nos. 331, 342, 343, 357, and 366. All Mr. Herbert Watkins's portraits are artistic and lifelike.

We turn now to a less pleasing portion of our task —the faults of photographs. These, like their merits, chiefly consist in choice of view, lighting, focussing, grouping, &c., and in all these respects instances may be pointed out which may act as beacons to the young adventurer in the art.

A common fault in choice of view is getting the principal object exactly into the centre, or, at all events, so near to it that the calculating faculty is at once aroused instead of the imaginative, and the spectator longs for a foot rule to ascertain whether the picture is exactly bisected or not. Instances of this may be seen in 197 and 295, the latter having the additional fault of facing the spectator full instead of a little obliquely, which is the more pity as Magdalen Tower presents so many much better aspects from other directions. In No. 120 a very curious effect is produced by the absence of all the usual standards of measurement, for want of which the spectator can scarcely avoid taking the edging to the flower-borders for the height of ordinary railings, and so raising the windows above into gigantic proportions.

Bad lighting is another very common fault; this may be studied in Nos. 67 and 135, the latter giving one the idea of the fish having been left out till so late at night that the forgetful sportsman is forced to bring a lantern to look for them.

But it is in grouping that the chief difference lies between the artist and the mere chemical manipulator, and melancholy instances of what may be done in this way are only too easy to point out. Mr. Robinson's groups are usually exquisite, and some of his have already been noticed as such; but in No. 68 not only has the head of the principal figure been thrown out of focus for the sake of other parts of the picture, but the infant has been so placed that its feet are terribly magnified, giving it the effect of a hideous dwarf. The same remark applies to 459, where this group is repeated, though the effect is rather less apparent from the diminution of the picture. Mr. Robinson has also inflicted a pair of very large feet on the central figure in 98, a picture otherwise admirable. In No. 183 he has thrown all three figures into strained and unlikely attitudes, while the eyes of the right-hand girl would most certainly be fixed on the spectator, who is necessarily close upon the group. In No. 142 there is a unity of attention given to the group, but it is centred on nothing; the eye involuntarily wanders over the pile of logs in search of the figure of the stump orator or field preacher who *ought* to be there, but whose motions appear to have been too continuous and energetic for photography to catch him. In 501 the figures, though practised actors, are greatly wanting in life and meaning; but perhaps the crowning instance of what may be achieved by a resolutely stiff and conventional arrangement may be found in No. 537. A resigned gloom has settled over nearly all the unfortunate victims; and if the second picture from the right in the top row were only labelled " Entrance to a Panoramic Exhibition, all the seats full, and no view to be had from the door," it would be indeed excellent.

One other fault, but much less common than any of the preceding, remains to be noticed—the attempting of manifest impossibilities. Some instances of this may be found in Mr. Piper's beautiful pictures, where, by taking a point of view too near for the powers of the lens, a disagreeable pyramidal effect is given to the buildings—see Nos. 44, 51, and 196. This effect may be especially noticed in 244, where the buildings actually appear to be falling. In 198 and 305 effects are attempted which cannot possibly be all in focus at once, and a woolliness of effect is inevitable.

Mr. Paul Pretsch's nature engraving is interesting, though the result is so uniformly dark as to be hardly satisfactory.

I have omitted to mention some fine views of Niagara Falls exhibited by the London Stereoscopic Company. Through an oversight, probably, they are not numbered in the catalogue, but they nevertheless are well worthy the attention of the visitor. I would especially mention " The General View of Niagara," embracing the Horseshoe Fall, Goat Island, and the American Fall.

THE LOUNGER.

BLOOD

Tempests whistling,
Thorn-brakes bristling,
    Blood !
Moonlight glinting,
Felons squinting,
Burglars hinting
      Murder ! Blood !

Storm-birds battling,
Hailstones rattling,
    Blood !
Earthquakes shaking,
Mountains quaking,
Whirlwinds raking.
      Murder ! Blood !

Ruffians slaying,
Bloodhounds baying,
    Blood !
Pistols shotted,
Bludgeons knotted,
Men garotted,
      Murder ! Blood !

BLOOD

Sword-blades pointed,
Limbs disjointed,
   Blood!
Cripples wallowing,
Gurgling, swallowing,
Vainly holloing
   Murder! Blood!

Thunder bursting,
Witches thirsting
   Blood!
Mandrakes creaking,
Pale ghosts shrieking,
Vampires seeking
   Murder! Blood!

Witch-yells dinning,
White skulls grinning,
   Blood!
Eye-balls flashing,
Jawbones gnashing,
All things smashing,
   Murder! Blood!

LINES

[To a friend at Radley College, who had complained " that I was glad enough to see him when he came, but didn't seem to care about it if I stayed away."]

AND cannot pleasures, while they last,
Be actual, unless, when past,
They leave us shuddering and aghast,
  With anguish smarting?
And cannot friends be fond and fast,
  And yet bear parting?

And must I then, at Friendship's call,
Calmly resign the little all—
(Trifling, I grant, it is, and small—)
  I have of gladness,
And lend my being to the thrall
  Of gloom and sadness?

And think you that I should be dumb,
And full " dolorum omnium,"
Excepting when you choose to come
  And share my dinner?
At other times be sour, and glum,
  And daily thinner?

188

Must he then live in groans and screams,
Who'd prove himself the friend he seems,
And haunt, by day, all silent streams,
    At night sleep badly,
Oft muttering in his broken dreams
    The name of Radley?

The lover, if, for certain days,
His fair one be denied his gaze,
Sinks not in grief and wild amaze,
    But, wiser wooer,
He spends the time in writing lays,
    And posts them to her.

And if he be an Oxford Don,
Or " Jonson's learned sock be on,"
A touching Valentine anon
    The post shall carry,
When thirteen days are come and gone
    Of February.

189

Farewell, dear friend, and when we meet
Here in my rooms, or in the street,
Perhaps before this week shall fleet,
    Perhaps to-morrow,
I trust to find *your* heart the seat
    Of wasting sorrow.
CH: CH: Feb: 1860.

LAYS OF MYSTERY, IMAGINATION, AND HUMOUR

BLOGGS' WOE

WHEN on the sandy shore I sit,
   Beside the salt sea-wave,
And fall into a weeping fit
   Because I dare not shave,
A little whisper at my ear
Enquires the reason of my fear.

I answer " if that ruffian, Jones,
   Should recognize me here,
He'd bellow out my name in tones
   Offensive to the ear:
He chaffs me so on being stout,
   A thing that always put me out."

Ah me! I see him on the cliff:
   Farewell, farewell to hope,
If he should look this way, and if
   He's got his telescope!
To whatsoever place I flee,
My hated rival follows me!

For it has happened once or twice
    I've met him out at dinner,
Just as I've come across a nice
    Party, and sworn to win her;
And he is slim, and I am stout,
And so he comes and cuts me out.

The girls (just like them!) all agree
    To praise J. Jones Esquire:
I ask them what on earth they see
    About him to admire;
They say "he is so sleek and slim,
It's quite a treat to look at him!"

They vanish in tobacco-smoke,
    Those visionary maids—
I feel a sharp and sudden poke
    Between the shoulder-blades—
"Why, Bloggs, my boy! You're getting stout!"
I told you he would find me out!

"My fat is not *your* business, Sir!"
    "No more it is, my boy!
But if it's *yours*, as I infer,
    Why, Bloggs, I give you joy!
A man, whose business prospers so,
Is just the sort of man to know.

" It's hardly safe, though, talking here,
   I'd best get out of reach :
For such a weight as yours, I fear,
   Must shortly sink the beach——"
Insult me thus because I'm stout!
I vow I'll go and call him out!

Nov. 1862.